THE HUNT FOR THE BOOK OF SECRETS

THE LAST TEMPLARS - BOOK 4

PRESTON W. CHILD

BOOKS BY PRESTON WILLIAM CHILD

All Books by Preston William Child in Order

http://prestonwilliamchild.com/books

SPECIAL OFFER

Want to read some of my books for FREE?
Available for a limited time only. To download them, go
to my

Free Starter Library

"The best way to find out if you can trust somebody is to trust them."

Ernest Hemingway

"Everything happens for a reason."

Dr. John Henry "Doc" Holiday

PROLOGUE

It was nearly 3:00 a.m. when Noah Allaman and his wife, Madeleine, stepped off their transatlantic flight at New York's JFK Airport. They were grateful to have finally completed the ten-hour leg of their journey from Edinburgh, Scotland, but they weren't looking forward to walking two concourses over to catch their six-and-a-half-hour connect flight to Montana.

"I'll run and grab us a couple of coffees if you take my bag," Madeleine proposed and flashed Noah a weary but still-dazzling smile.

Noah gladly accepted the bargain and hefted the oversized, leather Rnwen-STB travel duffel bag he'd bought for her a week before the trip. The fine leather carry-on was his expression of appreciation for her understanding of his need to make the grueling five-day roundtrip—and for her offering to go with him. So while his wife made a beeline to the coffee shop halfway up the concourse, Noah happily gripped the bag's rolled leather handles in his large left hand and casually headed in the same direction. In his right hand, he held the handle of the new 60-inch-long, carbon fiber hard case that contained the latest longsword he'd had custom-made by a swordsmith on Scotland's Isle of Sky.

"Well, looky what we have here!" he heard someone in a nearby gate area say. "It's a brother with a fancy rifle, all legal and shit!"

Noah kept walking but locked eyes with the lanky, brutish, young black man who'd made the remark from the two seats he was sprawled across. Two others who looked even younger and stronger rose to their feet along with the talker, and the three of them approached Noah as the last of his fellow passengers hustled by and left him on his own in the near-empty concourse. Noah hoped the three hoodlums merely wanted to have some fun at his expense—that they'd soon size him up as the tall, serious-looking, and powerfully-built specimen he was—then harmlessly move on. But he braced himself for the worst, just in case.

"A rifle in such a fancy case must be heavy and very expensive," the ringleader said with a sneer and reached for the case's handle. "Why don't you let me carry that for you, my brother?"

"It's not a rifle," Noah simply said without breaking stride.

"Well, that sure ain't holdin' pool sticks or a trombone,"

the ringleader said sarcastically. "So is it a shotgun, or an AK-47, or some shit like that?"

"It's a replica of the Fuilteach Mhuirt," Noah replied and kept walking.

"What the fuck is that?" the ringleader asked with a stupid grin.

"The largest claymore longsword ever made," Noah answered and kept walking.

"Longsword?" the ringleader sneered. "Motherfucker, I got the longest sword ever made right here," he said as he grabbed the crotch of his grimy jeans and his buddies cackled. "What the fuck did you call it?" the simpleton asked with one eye closed.

"Fuilteach Mhuirt," Noah repeated. "That's what the Scots have called the original since the early 15th century. It means 'Bloody One of Killing.'"

"You got a sword with a killer name?" the ringleader asked as he stepped directly into Noah's path and clicked open a switchblade knife. "Now I know it's expensive. So how 'bout you open that fancy case and show it to us? Lionel, hold the man's sweet-lookin' leather bag for him so he can show us his fancy sword."

Noah surrendered the bag and set about maintaining the trio's attention while Madeleine silently approached them from behind. She set the two coffees on the floor, then stood and grasped the grip of the deadly Bersa

Thunder .380 CC strapped under her left arm, inside her leather jacket.

But gunplay was the last thing Noah wanted inside an airport—especially JFK—and especially at 3:00 a.m. when TSA agents and airport security would be looking for something to keep them awake. He knew he couldn't risk looking past the trio and tipping them off about Madeleine's presence. So he moved in the opposite direction and laid the carbon fiber case across several seats in the gate area. He blocked the tumblers with his body as he dialed-in the combination. When he opened the case, the bright overhead lights gleamed off the 22-pound, 55-inch, hand-forged, razor-sharp work of art.

"You wasn't kiddin', motherfucker," the ringleader said and reached for the sword.

"Whoa, Big Daddy!" Noah said firmly and blocked the move with an outstretched arm.

"Who do you think you're talkin' to, cocksucker?" the creep asked and raised his knife.

"Who do you think is right behind you with a gun?" Madeleine asked firmly and aimed her powerful Argentine-made pistol at the ringleader. "I just bought this little beauty last week, and I'm absolutely dying to use it. Do any of you feel like dying if I have to use it?"

"Take it easy, pretty lady," the ringleader turned to her and said sweetly as he carefully put his knife away. "I just get a little carried away when I see beautiful things. You know how that it is, right?" he said and flashed Noah a sly smile.

"Leave now, or you will be carried away," Madeleine said ominously.

"Drop the gun, Mrs. Allaman!" a burly TSA agent barked from across the concourse, as two others pointed their pistols at the group. "Everyone put your hands up where I can see 'em!" he commanded.

Madeleine slowly laid the Bursa on the floor and raised her hands along with the others.

"Andy, my man!" the ringleader said with a grin. "Been a while since I seen you, man!"

"Not nearly long enough, Calvin," TSA Commander Andrew Mosely replied gruffly. "Looks like they neglected to block your access code when they fired your worthless behind in July. I'll make sure they correct that oversight as soon as they get in later this morning. But right now, I need to see everyone's ID and get good answers to a bunch of questions."

Noah closed the case and was about to spin the tumblers to relock it when Commander Mosely said, "Leave it open and show me your ID and passport, now, Mr. Allaman."

Noah reopened the case and carefully pulled his boarding passes, Swiss citizenship papers, and passport out of his jacket's inside pocket. Madeleine handed the burly commander her boarding passes, passport, and

Montana driver's license, along with her CCW permit. She and Noah both silently puzzled over how he knew their names. It was clear he'd crossed paths with the three losers before, but Madeleine and Noah were sure they'd never met him. They could see him relax as his colleagues hustled Calvin and his two buddies away.

"You can put that Bursa away now," he told Madeleine. "And Noah, please do lock that sword away. If I had to, I'd guess both weapons are work-related."

"That's a fair guess," Noah replied with a sigh of relief and handed the agent a business card with a phone number embossed into a photo of the White House. "If you call that number, I'm sure you'll get all the answers you need," he said simply.

Fifteen minutes later, Mosely hung up his office phone, handed Madeleine and Noah their papers back, and held his office door open for them.

"So, how did you know our names?" Noah just had to ask before they left.

"Facial Recognition software," Commander Mosely said simply and pointed to a computer monitor. "You've both been in our database for a couple a' years."

"Roger that!" Noah said with a knowing smile. "How about a lift to Gate 3C?"

"Gladly," the commander replied. "You do have one-way tickets, right?"

INTRODUCTION

Noah and Madeleine were exhausted when they finally settled into the otherwise empty first-class section aboard their nonstop flight to Montana and their own king bed. Noah gently covered Madeleine's hand with his and asked, "So how long do you think we've been in the TSA database, and what do you suppose it says about us?"

"Who knows? And what does it really matter?" Madeleine answered him. "Whatever information the TSA has, I'm sure they don't know the half of who we are and what we do," Madeleine reasoned. "And I suppose what information they do have is, at best, only half right."

"And you find comfort in that?" Noah asked her earnestly.

"I believe there's always an advantage in having people

wrongly think they know all they need to know about us," his wife said with her familiar, knowing smile. "So yes, I'm comfortable knowing most people just look at the river, with no thought of the sea."

"What does that mean?" Noah asked.

"People often miss the forest for the trees," Madeleine put it another way. "They can be quick to focus on a few details at the expense of missing the big picture. Take Commander Mosely, for instance. The minute he verified that we were who we said we were, that our papers were in order and that we have a White House connection, he couldn't have been happier to send us on our way. He even gave us a lift to our gate.

"Yet neither one of us carries any sort of official U.S. federal identification. Thanks to our passports, he knows you're a Swiss national, and I'm a citizen of France. But he doesn't know that less than two years ago, you were a student at the Florence School of Stadium Architecture. And he has no idea that I lived in Rome for three of the past five years as a full-time researcher in the Secret Library of the Holy See. Even if he did know those details, he still wouldn't have a clue—he may not even care—why we're both carrying deadly weapons through one of the busiest airports in the country in the middle of the night.

"He has no need to know, so he doesn't want to know. But if he did, we'd still be in his office answering questions instead of relaxing here in first class and preparing to order drinks."

"Good morning, ladies and gentlemen," a calm, resonant voice came over the intercom. "Welcome aboard American Airlines Flight 483. My name is William H. Walker, and I'm your captain for the six-and-a-half-hour flight to Glacier Park International Airport ..."

Madeleine and Noah suspended their conversation for the litany of routine preflight instructions and reminders recited by the captain and flight crew. Less than 20 minutes later, at more than 37,000 feet, Madeleine slipped her shoes off and reclined her seat just enough to stretch out while she sipped on the Four Roses bourbon and Coca Cola she'd ordered with a twist of lemon. Noah quickly drank a Frozen Chocolate Brandy Alexander and ordered another.

"Two?" Madeleine asked her husband. "That's not like you."

"Best I've ever had," he said with a slight chuckle. "They must use Swiss chocolate."

The drinks had the desired effect, and both members of "The President's Dozen" were fast asleep by the time their flight was over Wisconsin. Noah slept peacefully. But Madeleine wrestled with a dark dream in which she and Noah and the rest of the top-secret team battled with the most powerful and merciless adversaries they'd ever faced. In that fitful darkness, Madeleine wasn't even sure her adversaries were human. They wore black hoods and hid behind nightmarish Juggalo makeup. They were bloodthirsty and possessed superhuman strength that made them seem invincible. When Noah woke her a half-hour before their plane landed in Montana, she felt silly for being so frightened by a dream. But of course, she had no idea it would soon come true.

1

THINKING OF THE SEA

W hile Madeleine and Noah were still en route to Montana, President Donald Prescott sat sleepless in the White House. He'd been awake all night, mulling over possible responses to sensitive questions he figured he might be asked during his Daily Briefing with his Director of National Intelligence, Elaine Armstrong, in just a few hours. He was grateful that Armstrong had given him a heads-up the day before that she had asked Brett Reed, his newly confirmed Central Intelligence Agency director, and Rear Admiral Colin Walter Kramer, Commander of the Office of Naval Intelligence, to attend the briefing as well.

Armstrong had explained that she asked Kramer and Reed to participate in this particular briefing because they both had "a few routine questions" concerning facts surrounding some "mysterious events" that had occurred both on and off U.S. soil in recent months. So, as he always knew it would, the day had arrived when the nation's spymasters would begin trying to tie those events to the White House.

The president knew that there are no "routine questions" in matters of national security. Experience told him the trio probably wasn't as curious about the events as much as they wanted to make it clear to him that they expected to be kept advised of planned covert operations and the outcomes before they happen. Nevertheless, he wanted to have plausible answers—and plausible denials—ready for them.

The clock on his nightstand said 4:37 when the president rested his back against two firm buckwheat hull pillows he'd piled against the massive, hand-carved, dark cherry wood headboard of the Lincoln Bed. He texted his chief of staff, Jasper Cornwall, asking him to arrive at the White House an hour early that morning and join him for breakfast to discuss "a few things" before the president's Daily Briefing with Armstrong, Kramer, and Reed.

Though Cornwall knew a few facts related to some of the "mysterious events," he had no knowledge whatsoever about others. So the president needed to address his chief of staff's blind spots about the most critical of the operations before the two of them sat for the briefing. He hoped the questions Cornwall would have during their breakfast meeting would serve as a sort of dry run for the briefing. To help ensure as much, he also texted his chief of staff his best guesses concerning questions that might come up during the briefing.

- How exactly was the terrorist Abdul Rahman Yasin apprehended in Montana?
- Is there any truth to the rumor that an AWOL French Foreign Legionnaire was recently held at, and escaped from, the Guantanamo Bay Detention Camp?
- Why was Navy Captain Augustus Tucker Baird suddenly removed from the USS Ronald Reagan in the summer of 2016, and how was it accomplished?
- What's become of Navy Captain Baird's older brother, billionaire industrialist Jonah Baird, and was he involved in the captain's removal from the Reagan?
- Why did a Navy SEAL team go ashore at Acre, Israel, in early 2016, and was their mission successful?

It wasn't a complete list. But the president finally felt he could sleep. So he reclined in the massive bed Mary Todd Lincoln purchased in 1861 and drifted off while pondering what he was prepared to share with Armstrong, Kramer, and Reed ... and how much they might already know.

Three hours later, Jasper Cornwall was seated at the First Family's dining room table and had just finished scanning the front page of the *Washington Post* when the president bounded into the dining room wearing a dazzling smile and an equally dazzling light gray, hand-tailored, three-piece Scottish tweed Desmond Merrion Supreme Bespoke suit.

"Good morning, Mr. President," Cornwall said as he rose to his feet. "I watched you do it in high school and during six years of college. Hell, I did it myself back then every once in a while. But I sure as hell don't know how you can still do it."

"Good morning to you too, Jasper!" the president said with a curious look in his eye. "What are you talking about?"

"You were awake most of the night. I know you were," Cornwall replied. "I got your texts, and I could tell you'd been brooding over those questions. I could understand you not needing a lot of sleep when we were in ninth grade. But you're 74 years old now, for God's sake. It's time you got a good night's sleep."

"I get all the sleep I need," the president assured his best friend. "Have you ordered?"

"I was waiting for you," Cornwall answered as Winston, the head dining room attendant, approached the table. "Good morning, Winston!" Cornwall said. "I'd love a couple of poached eggs and three slices of lightly buttered raisin bread with black coffee. Thank you for the tomato juice you had waiting for me. How's the family? How's Stewart handling his first year at Pitt?"

"Everyone's doing wonderfully, Mr. Cornwall," Winston replied with a broad smile. "Stewart's adjusting to being away from home just fine, sir. Thank you for asking."

"Well, please tell him hello for Elaine and I," Cornwall said.

"I'll be sure to tell him," Winston said with an even broader smile. "He'll appreciate knowing you and Mrs. Cornwall are thinking of him. And what will you have this fine morning, Mr. President?"

"It's a steak morning, Winston, medium-rare, as always," the president said as he spread a large linen napkin across his lap and tucked another into the front of his collar.

"Two eggs or three this morning, Mr. President?" Winston asked quietly.

"Three, over easy," the president told him.

"Potatoes? Juice? Fruit?" Winston asked quickly.

"No to all three," the president replied. "Just protein this morning. I'm going to need it. And bring us two pots of coffee too, please."

"Coffee's comin' right up! I'll have the rest out here shortly, Mr. President," Winston said and headed to the kitchen.

"So, are you ready to tap dance this morning?" Cornwall asked with a sly grin.

"That'll be tough with my feet being held to the fire," the president chuckled warily.

"When it counts, Gregory Hines ain't got nothin' on you," Cornwall said with a grin.

"Call it tap-dancing if you want, Jasper," the president said defensively. "The media can bang the 'transparency' drum all they want. But you know very well that, in this job, the three secrets of success are knowing what to disclose, whom to disclose it to, and when."

When breakfast arrived, the coffee was poured, and the conversation began in earnest.

"So, what am I going to hear that I don't already know?" Cornwall asked bluntly.

"There's only one way to find out, Jasper," the president said enthusiastically. "Press me like we both know I'll be pressed in the briefing, and we'll see where it leads. It's a sure bet that they have more information than they'll let on. So I hope to learn at least as much from their questions as they learn from my answers.

"The trick will be to keep my answers short in order to hear as many of their questions as possible in the half-hour they will be in the Oval with us. Camilla will interrupt the briefing 30 minutes after it begins," the president continued. "I'll keep my answers short, and the clock will hopefully help me avoid disclosing too much."

"Ahhh, the classic Washington 'limited hangout,'" Cornwall noted. "How's that steak?"

"A limited hangout indeed—and the steak's perfect!" the president replied with a sly smile. "The vaguer my answers are during the briefing, the more questions those three will ask. And the more they talk, the less I'll have to."

"So you're planning a 'modified limited hangout,'" Cornwall said with another sly smile. "Richard Nixon would be proud. This could be fun."

"Perhaps," the president sighed. "But the odds are good that you'll hear a thing or two that you don't currently know about. After all, I have to keep some operations close to the vest for the sake of national security."

"Are you saying you don't have full confidence in our intelligence community … and in me?" Cornwall asked incredulously.

"Don't take it personal, Jasper," the president cautioned. "Some of the information is extremely sensitive. And the less you know about it, the less pressure you have to contend with. No pun intended—but it's no secret that our intelligence community has very real challenges concerning their ability to safeguard information critical to our national interest. You know as well as I do how they leak and withhold information to suit their purposes. Operational and political realities must constantly be reconciled. Meanwhile, there are also diplomatic realities. We've got allies that must be considered—and potential allies that ask to be considered."

"Easy, Mr. President!" Cornwall said. "I don't need

convincing. We're on the same page. But dealing with Armstrong. Reed and Kramer might bring a whole different chapter. So let's do a quick run-through of your list of questions."

The president and his chief of staff used the remaining few minutes to discuss "safe" responses to the anticipated questions then headed downstairs to the West Wing. They found Armstrong, Kramer, and Reed sitting restlessly around Camilla's desk outside the Oval Office, and she was unsuccessfully trying to engage them in light conversation.

"Good morning, everyone!" the president said in his usual booming morning voice and glanced at his watch without breaking stride as he led the way into the Oval. "Sorry to keep you waiting, but we're right on schedule nonetheless. It's good to see you, Brett. How was your first week at the agency?"

"A little hectic, to say the least, but just fine, Mr. President," Reed told him.

"Hectic is good," the president said with a friendly smile as he sat behind the Resolute Desk. "That's the CIA's 'normal.'"

"And how are the both of you this morning?" he asked Armstrong and Kramer.

"Just fine, as always, Mr. President," Armstrong said as she entered the combination into the lock on the attaché containing five iPads, and passed them out.

"I'm fine as well, Mr. President," Kramer said.

"We have a lot of ground to cover. So I'd like to get started if I may," Armstrong said.

"That's what we're all here for," the president said and cast a slight smile at Cornwall.

The moment all users' retinal scans were completed, they clicked on the "PBD" icon, and a small digital clock at the bottom of each iPad screen displayed the time to the hundredth of a minute. The president quickly initiated his iPad because he knew the clock on the first screen to come alive started a second clock that ticked off the elapsed time of the briefing on each of the other screens. As his clock began, the president settled into his chair and took a slow, deep breath.

"Well, what have you got for us today?" he asked the group.

"We've scrapped the planned topics in order to brief you on an alarming overnight development, Mr. President," Armstrong said and tapped a link that started a slide show on each of the iPad screens. "Admiral Kramer will explain."

"Mr. President, China's nuclear-powered 'Hidden Dragons' came out of hiding last night," the admiral said. "We captured satellite images of several nuclear Type 094A Jin Class subs as they exited the top-secret underground hangar at Yulin Naval Base on Hainan Island."

"How many is 'several'?" the president shot back.

"That's the worst of it," Kramer told him. "All previous intelligence had us believing the Chinese had just six of these monsters. But as you can see, there are twice that many in last night's images alone. They had to know we'd see this flotilla. And experience tells us this is President Liú's way of letting us know this is not the entire 094A fleet."

"These are their deadliest fish, right?" the president asked.

"By a longshot, Mr. President," Kramer said emphatically.

"How much do we know about them, specifically?" President Prescott pressed him.

"The 094A is armed with 12 JL-3 MIRVs, each loaded with a one-megaton nuclear warhead and an estimated range of 9,000 kilometers," the admiral explained. "So an 094A sailing just northeast of the Kuril Islands in the South China Sea could strike any target in the contiguous United States. Fortunately for us, the subs are noisy. So we'll hear them before they get close enough. But India's on their doorstep and doesn't have listening technology."

"Then it's time they did," the president said emphatically and told Cornwall. "Make sure that's close to the top of the agenda for next week's meeting with the Joint Chiefs."

"Got it! What the hell's a MIRV?" Cornwall asked in an effort to follow along.

"A multiple independently-targetable re-entry vehicle," the admiral explained. "It could spell disaster if the Chinese conquer the 094A's noise issues. With this many 094As, they could theoretically launch surprise first-strike attacks on India, Russia, and the U.S simultaneously."

"President Liú restated China's 'No-First-Use' pledge when he visited here last summer," the president noted. "So what does all this mean, realistically?"

"It means there's a whole lot the Chinese are not telling us," the admiral said ominously. "For starters, it means the caverns they've dug under that mountain on Hainan Island are far larger than we thought. That likely means their nuclear warhead storage capability is also far larger. Did President Liú happen to mention anything about that during his visit?"

"Of course not. Why would the People's Republic of China act any differently than any other nation?" the president asked rhetorically. "Have we redeployed our hydrophone arrays? I want to ensure we hear every move those fish make."

"Redeployment began at 0500, Mr. President," the admiral assured him. "Currently, the subs appear to be headed for routine exercises."

"Excellent," the president shot back. "I want to know

immediately if that changes. In the meantime, please share these images with the Situation Room."

"You can count on it, Mr. President," the admiral again assured him.

"That's all we have for today's briefing," Armstrong announced. "As I indicated to you yesterday, we do have a few questions for you about other matters."

President Prescott wasn't at all surprised that the briefing, which typically lasted 45 to 60 minutes, took just 16.58 minutes, despite the groundbreaking revelations concerning the Chinese submarine program. In fact, he was thrilled and confident he could "tap dance" around the questions to come for the remaining time ... provided Camilla interrupted the briefing as planned.

"Thanks for keeping me on top of this, Admiral Kramer," the president said. "Now, I'm anxious to hear everyone's questions."

Cornwall looked down at his shoes to hide the smirk on his face.

The admiral asked the first question while Armstrong collected the iPads and returned them to the attaché for the 13-mile return trip to DNI headquarters in McClean, Virginia, where their memories would be wiped clean and prepped for the next day's briefing.

"Mr. President," the admiral began, "is there any truth to the rumor that an AWOL French Foreign Legionnaire was recently held at Gitmo and that he and an

American citizen who was also being held there briefly escaped into the U.S.?"

"Well, admiral," the president said with a determined look and calm voice, "I'm sure you're aware of the Guantanamo Bay Detention Camp's record of never having allowed anyone to escape since it was established in 2002."

"Sources have recently indicated to us that that's no longer the case," the admiral replied.

"Well, sources can be wrong," the president replied slyly, "as we discussed just moments ago concerning things as difficult to miss as submarines that are more than 400 feet long."

"So are you saying the camp did not recently detain a French Foreign National?" the admiral asked specifically.

"No, I'm not," the president finally conceded. "But I am saying that the individual was returned to France after being held less than 24 hours at Guantanamo at that nation's request."

"Such use of the camp is highly irregular," the admiral asserted.

"But it is within the camp's charter, and it was done at the request of French President Andre DuPris, who asked that we hold the Legionnaire just long enough for his government to arrange his safe return to France. We agreed to nothing more and nothing less."

That's the best limited hangout I've ever heard, Cornwall thought to himself. *Factual and unequivocal, with no lies or misdirection ... while not completely forthcoming.*

CIA Director Reed changed the subject by asking why a Navy SEAL team reportedly went ashore at Acre, Israel, in early 2018.

"That was some time ago," the president said just as he had earlier to Cornwall. "That operation was ordered by me and is still highly classified. But I assure you that the Israeli government was consulted prior to our team going ashore. I can also assure you that at no time did any SEAL team member interact with an Israeli citizen or a member of the Israeli military. As a matter of fact, that country's general population is still unaware that the operation occurred. Is that everything?"

"Not quite," Admiral Kramer told him. "What were the circumstances surrounding Navy Captain Augustus Baird's sudden removal from command of the USS Ronald Reagan in the summer of 2016, and how was it accomplished?"

"I'm sorry, but as long ago as that operation occurred, I still can't discuss it," the president replied. "The Naval Criminal Investigative Service has classified the details related to the matter as Sensitive Compartmented Information. As you probably already know, admiral, the NCIS ultimately accepted my recommendation that Captain Baird be granted full retirement status and retain his security clearances in recognition of his decades of distinguished service and conspicuous bravery under fire in numerous hostile naval engagements.

"I can tell you that Captain Baird is doing extremely well in retirement, despite the recent passing of his wife," the president said. "In fact, I guess it's not premature of me to tell you that I'm considering him for the position of my Senior Advisor for Strategic Military Affairs."

Whoa! Cornwall shouted in his head upon hearing the off-the-cuff announcement.

"That news makes my questions all the more timely and important," Armstrong told the president as she secured the attaché containing the iPads using a diamond-cut, carbon steel chain locked to an attractive platinum bracelet she tightened around her slender left wrist.

"What, if anything, can you tell us about the disappearance of Captain Baird's older brother, Jonah Baird? Is it true that he was aboard the helicopter that exploded and crashed into the Hudson River south of Manhattan last month?"

"I wish I had something I could share with you about that," the President sighed as he leaned back into his high-backed chair. "It's all still under investigation by the New York Port Authority and the FBI. But I give you my word that I'll update you the moment I can."

"What do you know about media reports of rumored FBI leaks that link him to a small band of mercenaries, a number of whose members have been questioned and/or detained by local law enforcement here and abroad over the past year and a half or so?" she asked.

Camilla, where are you? the president thought to himself but resisted the temptation to look at his watch.

"Well, to start with," he replied to Armstrong, "I'm very frustrated by what has become a plague of leaked information—most of which is incorrect, by the way—reportedly coming out of the Bureau and other federal agencies and offices. It's not helpful in our efforts to be transparent, and it dishonors the efforts of good and decent Americans who are on highly sensitive, and sometimes quite dangerous, assignments both here at home and overseas."

Come on, Camilla! Cornwall shouted inside his brain. He stole a glance at the tall case clock standing beside the door that connects the Oval and her office, and he hoped the president wouldn't have to "tap dance" much longer.

"But to address the alleged FBI leak, in particular, I'm currently unable to confirm or deny its accuracy. The story makes for entertaining conjecture, but seems very farfetched."

"Well, can you at least confirm whether or not he had any input into the decision to remove his brother from command of the *Ronald Reagan*?"

"Ummm…" the President began to answer.

"I'm sorry to interrupt, Mr. President," Camilla's voice said over the intercom on the president's desk, "but the call you told me to expect is on the other line and sounds urgent."

"Thank you, Camilla!" the president said, then rose from his chair and announced, "I'm very sorry to cut our time short today. But I really must take this call. So please excuse me."

Armstrong, Kramer, and Reed rose from their chairs along with Cornwall and the president and followed Cornwall out of the Oval with only a little more information than they had when the briefing began. Cornwall thanked the trio for coming, walked them out the North entrance, and hustled back to the Oval to applaud the president's successful "tap dance."

"Well done!" he cheerfully told the president, who stood looking out a window and did not reply. "You surprised me with the Baird appointment," Cornwall added, but the president still didn't reply. "But we can discuss that later if you like. What are you looking at?" he asked.

"I'm looking at the river," the president said softly.

"Looking at the river?" Cornwall asked, confused. "You can't see it from here."

"Oh, I can see it alright," the president quietly replied, still staring out the window.

"You've lost me," Cornwall sighed, certain he had no idea what the president meant.

"It's a haunting line in an old song by singer/composer Randy Newman," the president said as he finally moved away from the window and returned to his chair behind the large, imposing Resolute Desk. "Madeleine Allaman turned me on to him a while back, and that line from one of his songs gripped my mind as I pondered the briefing you and I just sat through."

"Now you've really lost me," Cornwall said as he pulled a chair close to the Resolute.

"It's a deep yet simple thought, really," the president explained. "Facts, like people, are what they are. What matters is how we see them. Most folks are content with the small picture, with knowing the basics. But if you want to see the big picture and fully understand facts and people, you have to know as much about them as you possibly can. It can be daunting with facts ... and nearly impossible with people."

"Keep going," Cornwall pleaded. "I think I almost know what you're talking about."

"Armstrong, Kramer, and Reed brought facts to our meeting in the hope of getting more," the president continued. "So did we. And we all managed to do exactly that. Now I'm hoping they're content to have the few facts I gave them. But as for me, I'll spend hours thinking over what they told me, what they asked me, and what it all tells me about the facts I had when they arrived, and how much I can trust the facts I now have ... and the people I got them from. I'll be looking at the river ... but thinking of the sea."

"Okay, but while you're looking and thinking, you've got a full schedule ahead that will keep you busy well into the evening," Cornwall said. "And to kick it off, you have a one-hour meeting with the two dozen local police chiefs you had me invite for a face-to-face. After that, you owe the press corps the 15 minutes you promised them earlier this week. Then ..."

"Stop," the president said gently. "Just keep me on course and on schedule as we go."

"It will be my pleasure, Mr. President," Cornwall said. "After all, I've been doing that since our junior year in high school."

"And look where it's gotten us," the president quipped. "Keep up the good work!"

2

U.S. Marshal Quinton "Q" Marshall was no stranger to harrowing car rides. He'd been on plenty of high-speed chases for more than 30 years in law enforcement. So he preferred rides to be safe and relaxing. But they were neither when he rode with his best friend, John Henry "Doc" Holiday, behind the wheel. Doc never seemed to have any idea—or even care—what the speed limit was. No matter what vehicle he drove, the tires—and his passengers—frequently made noise as he rounded corners. And it was sometimes worse on open roads.

"Don't you think it might be a good idea to slow down a bit?" Q asked not-so-subtly. "This new buggy is barely past its break-in mileage, and the boys' flight isn't due to arrive for another hour."

"Since when are you worried about my vehicles or the Byrnes brothers' schedule?" Doc chuckled as he backed off the gas pedal of his gleaming new 2021 Cadillac

Escalade Platinum. "You're not getting old on me, are you, Q?"

"Not yet. But I'd like to," Q replied with a relieved grin. "It's fine with me if a 25-minute ride takes 20 or 21 minutes. But 15 minutes is beyond my comfort level."

"Point made," Doc sighed. "But I do love this black beauty."

"You mean this 'Black Raven' beauty," Q said as a jab at carmakers. "Personally, I'm partial to 'Dark Moon Blue Metallic.' What do you think ever happened to ordinary colors?"

"Carmakers figured out people will pay more for fancier color names," Doc chuckled.

"So what brings the Byrnes brothers to Montana, anyway?" Q asked.

"Well, Tom said he wants us to see something and bounce a few questions off of us," Doc answered. "It sounded to me like he and Ray suspect they might have stumbled onto a rogue cell of Guardians outside Sedona this past week."

"You're kidding me!" Q shot back. "You always said the Guardians would scatter if we stopped Jonah Baird. And we sent him to the bottom of the Hudson River over a month ago."

"Well, we only know that he went into the Hudson ... Gravesend Bay to be exact," Doc said. "Divers still haven't recovered his body. And assuming he did go to the bottom, I guess it's only natural that there are jackals among his Guardians who are eager to get their hands on whatever money he might have stashed around the world."

"You gotta know he stashed a lot of money," Q agreed. "And I guess Sedona's as likely a place to look for it as any. Baird did have them carve out quite a stronghold there for him and that whacko Foreign Legionnaire pal of his. And thanks to us, they left there in a big hurry."

"So did we," Doc added. "Or have you forgotten that part?"

"Yeah, but we accomplished our mission," Q replied with a satisfied grin.

"Sorta," Doc said quietly and stared at the road ahead.

"What? You're still bummed out about Baird taking the flash drive to the bottom of the Hudson with him? Let it go, Doc. Our mission was to ensure bad people didn't end up with it."

"That might have been your mission, Q," Doc said, still staring straight ahead. "Mine was to hand it to the president."

"Come on, Doc!" Q said in exasperation. "The French got their Legionnaire back. We made sure the information on that flash drive will never get into the wrong hands. Jonah Baird's not going to harm anyone ever again. And we all went home alive. But all that's not good enough for you?!"

"Sending Chastain back to France in one piece was a home run," Doc conceded. "But the rest feels more like foul balls at best—except, of course, the part about all of us going home safe."

"It ain't baseball, Doc," Q told his friend. "It's life or death. And so far, we're winning."

"Well, look who's become 'Mr. Positive' in his old age!" Doc said in mock surprise.

"Like I said earlier, I'm not old yet," Q snapped back at his friend. "And I'm about as positive a person as you'll ever meet. If I weren't, I wouldn't have set out on half the missions we've accepted."

"So, you're admitting that you don't come along just to protect me?" Doc asked wryly.

"That's a big part of the reason, for sure," Q said, sitting up straight in his seat. "But I've always been positive about my being just the man to do it."

"Oh, I see," Doc chuckled. "You mostly tag along just to keep me out of harm's way."

"Mostly, yeah," Q agreed. "I gotta do what I can to protect the few good friends I have. Why else would a man of my many talents resort to doing the kinds of things we do?"

"I guess there's a compliment in there somewhere," Doc

laughed.

"Does that mean you're gonna stop fishing for one?" Q laughed with him, then said, "Concentrate on the road, would ya, Doc? We're almost at the airport."

Doc and Q picked up the Byrnes brothers on the curb outside the terminal and headed back to the lake house to reunite them with the team for welcome conversation that would last late into the night.

"It's great to see you both again! How have you two been?" Thomas asked happily as he gripped Doc and Q by their shoulders from the back seat.

"Oh, we're makin' it just fine," Q replied as Doc hit the gas and headed back to Route 2. "Life's been a little boring since we last saw you fellas, of course. But we're makin' it just fine."

"Oh, right!" Raymon huffed with a grin. "Judging by the time we spent with you and the team on the Georgia coast not long ago, you're lucky if you have a couple of boring minutes in a month."

"So did you fly up here in search of excitement, or did you bring some with you?" Doc asked as he sped back to Flathead Lake.

"A little of both, you might say," Thomas answered as he watched the scenery race by. "I'm officially up here on business. But knowing how much fun we'll probably have, Ray insisted on coming along just for the fun of it."

"We're glad you both came," Q assured the brothers. "The team's anxious to see you both again. You better be hungry, 'cause they've put out quite a spread back at the house."

"I'm starving!" Thomas said.

"That makes two of us!" Raymon chimed in. "How long before we get there?"

"It normally takes 25 to 30 minutes," Q told him. "But with Doc behind the wheel, we'll be there in less than 15. You fellas do have your seat belts on, don't you?"

"Q, you're driving next time," Doc joked and saw on the navigation screen they were just 11 minutes from the lake house.

"S'okay with me," Q replied. "But I don't have a fancy buggy like this."

"That's because you hate to part with your money," Doc joked some more.

"I'm saving for retirement," Q told him.

"You can't retire," Thomas interjected. "It just wouldn't be the same without you."

"You can say that again," Raymon added. "You two are like the Lone Ranger and Tonto."

"Like Batman and Robin," Thomas asserted.

"Like Sherlock Holmes and Dr. Watson," Raymon kept it going.

"We're probably closer to Beavis and Butt-Head," Q chuckled.

"Speak for yourself," Doc said. "I like to think of us as Buzz Lightyear and Woody."

"That fits," Q chuckled. "I like wearin' Stetsons, and you're a space cadet!"

Doc pulled the big, black Escalade in front of the lake house and led the others up the broad steps and into the house where the crowd was waiting for them.

"Hello!" they all shouted when Raymon and Thomas entered the house.

"My gosh! You folks can sure make a person feel appreciated," Raymon said as he took in the welcome fragrances of pot roast and apple pie.

"Connie, do you have a sister who's single and cooks like you?" Thomas asked Doc's wife with a smile. "I'm tryin' to get my brother married off so our mom can stop worrying about him."

"Sorry, Tom," Doc chuckled. "She's an only child, and I plan on keeping her."

"You better!" Connie said with her trademark smile as she stepped forward and hugged the brothers. "Welcome to both of you!"

Marsha hugged them next, followed by Madeleine and Noah, and Louis and Jenny Danforth. After a bit more conversation and being shown their rooms, the brothers and the others all crowded around the long, solid oak dining room table and began passing food and small talk to one another.

When Doc had eaten his fill of Connie's world-class pot roast, he sat back in his chair and reveled in the peace and happiness of the setting, the friendship, and laughter that filled the house just as he and Connie had envisioned it when they had the large fieldstone and timber cottage built on the highest bluff overlooking Flathead Lake.

Once the eating slowed and the conversation grew quiet, Doc couldn't resist using the time before dessert to get down to business. He lightly tapped his wine glass with his fork to get everyone's attention.

"I promise not to monopolize our time with these two," he began. "But I'm curious about the excitement you said you brought for us here in the Treasure State, Tom."

"Have you got it on you?" Ray asked his brother from across the table.

"I do," Tom answered and pulled a wide, thick, ornate sterling silver ring from the left breast pocket of the fishing vest he was wearing. Though the ring was inside a small Ziplock evidence bag, it gleamed brightly when he held it out over the table, and it reflected the light from the large mule deer antler chandelier that hung overhead.

"Wow!" Doc said with genuine surprise. "That's quite a chunk of silver! Can I see it?"

"Of course," Tom said. "It's the main reason we're here."

"I thought the main reason was my charming personality," Q quipped.

"I thought it was my pot roast," Connie joined in with another smile.

Tom passed it to Jenny, who held it long enough to glimpse its design before passing it to the others, who each did the same until it finally reached Doc.

"May I take it out?" Doc asked.

"By all means," Tom told him. "We've run all our tests on it, and I'm hoping someone at this table might be able to add to what little we know about it."

"What do you know about it?" Doc asked as he inspected it closely.

"Well interestingly, it's strikingly similar to Heinrich Himmler's sterling silver Nazi SS Honor Ring," Tom said.

"Where'd you get it?" Doc asked, still staring at the ring he held at eye level.

"A bank robbery suspect we took into custody in Phoenix was wearing it," Tom told him.

"'To Alta Ali from L. Mancini,'" Doc read out loud as

he squinted at the inscription inside the band and then asked, "Is your suspect's name Ali or Mancini?"

"Ali. But it was Mancini that rang a bell with me," Tom said. "So, I did a little digging."

"And what did you find out?" Doc asked.

"INTERPOL questioned a guy named Lorenzo Manini in the murder of author, Culver Ainsley, in Rome nearly three years ago, remember?" Tom asked. "Mancini had a 'Guardian' tattoo on the inside of his left wrist, which linked him to the Keeper's Guardians. That was the clue that helped us understand that the Keeper had an international hit list of artists and authors."

"I do remember," Doc replied. "But Mancini's not an uncommon name."

"You're right," Scott shot back. "But as far as we know, only the Keeper's Guardians have 'Guardian' tattooed inside their left wrist. And Alta Ali has one."

"You have a Guardian in custody for a recent bank heist?" Doc asked in surprise.

"Well, we knew they'd have to find a new line a work with Baird out of the picture," Q jumped into the conversation. "Can I see that ring a minute, please?" he asked.

Doc passed it to Q, who looked at it intently.

"I know a guy who collects World War II relics, and he has one of those silver SS rings," Q said. "This does remind me of it. But it's not exactly like it, and it looks brand new."

"I just got a bad feeling about it when I saw 'L. Mancini' inscribed inside it," Tom said, almost apologetically. "Maybe I overreacted when I saw the Guardian tattoo. No one else in our office seemed interested. But no one else at the Phoenix office knows as much as we know about the Keeper and his Guardians."

"May I have a look at it?" Madeleine asked.

Q passed it to her, and Tom began to brace himself for the possibility that he might feel foolish by the time he went to bed later that evening. Madeleine studied the ring closely, spun it and turned and spun it, and turned some more.

"See anything important?" Doc asked her, knowing that if there was even the slightest clue that they should be concerned about, Madeleine would see it.

"The raised skull and crossbones are unquestionably similar to those on the Honour Ring that Heinrich Himmler presented to Hitler's senior SS commanders as a sort of morale booster," Madeleine said as she studied the ring very closely. "Each ring had the recipient's name, the presentation date, and Himmler's name engraved on the interior. And oddly enough, he insisted that it be worn only on the ring finger of the left hand."

"That's where Ali wore it!" Tom blurted out. "I'm sorry," he said. "Please go on."

"Himmler told recipients the ring was a reminder that they should be ready at all times to risk their lives for the life of the NAZI cause," Madeleine explained. "The rings were highly sought after and couldn't be bought or sold. Some SS members who didn't receive one from Himmler actually had local jewelers make replicas for them to wear. What interests me most, though, is the inscription. The presenter's name on this one is 'L. Mancini.' Himmler used only his first initial inside Honor Rings to save room for recipients' full names."

"Madeleine, how on earth do you know so much about so many things?" Q asked her.

"Hang around one of the world's largest and oldest libraries of historical texts, and you're bound to learn a thing or two," Madeleine said with a shrug.

"Unlike Honor Rings, this ring is 92.5 percent silver. It has no presentation date, but this one can't be more than a couple of weeks old. And it's not too big a leap to surmise that the 'L' in 'L. Mancini' stands for Lorenzo … and that he's mimicked Himmler's grisly 'Totenkopfring' to boost morale among his Guardians."

"What did you just call it?" Tom asked.

"'Totenkopfring,'" Madeleine repeated in perfect German and then translated it into perfect English. "That was its nickname among SS officers: 'The Death's Head Ring.'"

"Well, that's calling a spade a spade, in English and German!" Q blurted out.

"Yep," Madeleine agreed. "And because this ring is very obviously new, my guess is that the Guardian legion is alive and well … and death has a new ring."

Madeleine's conclusions were met with several seconds of stares and palpable silence.

"Damn it," Doc finally muttered, dropped his head, and rubbed the back of his neck. "Will this never end?" he asked no one in particular. And no one answered.

Connie played the ace up her sleeve, hoping to break the mood for at least a little while.

"Okay, folks!" she announced. "Time for dessert! Who wants their pie a' la mode?"

"Geez! English, German, and French in one conversation," Q quipped.

"Why don't you throw in some Polish for us, Quinton?" his wife, Marsha, asked him as she rose from her chair to help Connie serve dessert.

"You speak Polish?" Doc asked his friend, incredulously.

"I don't tell you everything, Doc," Q said with a smile.

Connie glanced out the doorway that led to the large deck off the dining room.

"Let's have dessert out under the stars," she suggested.

As the group moved outside, Doc took Q aside and quietly told him, "I'd give my left arm to have been wrong about the Guardians tonight."

"And I'd give mine to know which part of the theory you talked about on the way to the airport today, in fact," Q added. "On one hand, Baird may have somehow survived that crash into the bay. On the other hand, he may be fish food, and this Mancini fella might have accessed some, or all, of Baird's fortune and decided to take command of the Guardians instead of simply cutting them all loose and keeping the money for himself."

"I really hoped this nightmare was over," Doc said with his face pointed to the starlit sky. "I've told Connie several times that Baird's death meant we—and the rest of the world—could relax and life was back to normal. But if Madeleine's right about what that ring means, the Guardians aren't just snakes—they're a Hydra that refuses to die. That's a nightmare I don't want to give my life—or any team member's life—for.

"As a matter of fact," Doc added in an angry tone, "while we're here wrestling with the question of what is and isn't true, I'm wondering how much the president might already know and just hasn't told us. You and I are both experienced in water recovery. Baird went into Gravesend Bay a month ago. It's only 20 feet deep, and we still don't have his body. Does that seem likely to you? I've been asking myself what's taking so long for weeks now!

"I understood the need for secrecy when our mission to end Baird's global murder spree began. The president knew our intelligence community was leaky, and Baird was very well-connected in Washington. He used his fortune to form and finance the Guardians to do his dirty work and fuel his sick obsession to build his so-called Forbidden Library. I felt our team was a little responsible for that because we found the Lost Treasure of the Knights Templar for him, which enabled him to launch his insane scheme in the first place. And I don't even want to think about how we were sucked into chasing down that so-called Nostradamus and his 'lost scrolls.'

"But if Baird's dead, it's a whole new ball game as far as I'm concerned. So I almost don't care anymore. A part of me just wants to pack it all in and tell the president he can take it from here. Do you want to know the very worst of it?" Doc asked Q in exasperation.

"That's a rhetorical question if ever I've heard one," Q replied, hoping Doc would smile.

"The sum of all these parts has me worried about how much of all this has really been in our nation's interest … and how much of it is in President Prescott's political interest," Doc said. "Now that he's in the heat of his re-election campaign, he's avoiding embarrassment like the plague. How embarrassing do you think all this would be, exactly?"

"Whoa, partner!" Q said urgently. "You've got that cart way out in front of the horse. I've known and worked with the president quite a while, and I've always felt I can trust him. I'm sure he withholds information when he feels he has to. And if he doesn't trust someone he's dealing with, he never volunteers answers to questions that aren't asked. But my experience tells me he trusts you completely. So I'm telling you that if you ask him straight questions, he'll give you straight answers—and then some—every time."

"So I guess it's time for another visit to the Oval," Doc said with a sigh.

"Sounds to me like you need one," Q agreed.

"I'll call the White House in the morning," Doc said and bumped fists with Q. "Thanks for listening."

"Ditto," Q simply replied.

"Hey, you two! Come have some dessert! The ice cream's melting," Connie interrupted with a dazzling smile that masked her concern for the expression she'd seen on her husband's face from across the deck.

"She's trying to make me fat," Doc finally smiled and told Q as they followed Connie back to the gathering on the far side of the deck.

"It's working," Q said and put an arm around Doc's shoulders. "But you're still the best at what you do. Don't ever doubt that, Doc. I'll have two scoops on my pie, please, Connie!"

3

THE SITUATION ROOM SITUATION

When Doc called the next morning, the president and Chief of Staff Jasper Cornwall had already had breakfast, finished that morning's Daily Briefing, and were talking during a walk at the far end of the south lawn of the White House.

"Good morning, Doc!" Camilla said cheerfully. "I hope this is a casual, happy call."

"Good morning to you, Camilla!" Doc replied. "It is, thank you. I guess you don't get too many of them."

"Oh, we get them now and then," Camilla chuckled. "But we can never get too many. President Prescott is here this morning, but I'm afraid he's unavailable at the moment. He and Jasper went for a brief walk out on the south lawn. But I'll be happy to take a message and have him call you back."

"That will be fine, Camilla," Doc replied. "Please just let

him know I called and that I'd like to speak with him briefly when he's available."

"I'll be happy to do that, Doc," Camilla answered. "I'd appreciate it if you would tell Connie I said hello, and I send her my best."

"I'll be sure to tell her soon as I get to the kitchen," Doc lied, because Connie knew he never called the president for "casual, happy" conversation, and he wasn't quite ready to tell her he was planning to leave for D.C. again. That's why he'd made the call near the middle of Flathead Lake during his morning rowing routine. He hoped the president would call back soon so he could iron out the trip details before he broke the news to Connie.

But as Doc ended the call, the president was more than 100 yards from the Oval Office, standing and talking with Cornwall beside the fountain. And Jasper had no idea why.

"Do we really need to be standing here, Mr. President?" Cornwall asked his lifelong friend plaintively. "The grass is still wet! If you had warned me, I would have worn my rain boots. I just bought these shoes. What are we doing out here anyway? I thought you said you had something important to talk about, and this is an odd place to do it."

"We need the background noise," the president said. "I want to be sure this conversation is off the record.

Everything said in the Oval is taped. You know that. I have to speak frankly."

"But there are places to do that inside," Cornwall countered.

"Are there?" the president shot back. "Are you sure of that? I'm not."

"Since we're speaking frankly, you're beginning to worry me," Cornwall told him. "First, you hardly said a word during breakfast this morning, which you asked me to have with you for the second day in a row. Do you know what time I have to get up to be here for that? Then you refused to ask or take questions during the Daily Briefing. What's going on?"

"I'm not sure what's going on, Jasper," the president said sincerely. "And we have to figure out how to change that."

"What are you talking about, exactly?" Cornwall replied.

"I'm not sure of that either," the president answered earnestly. "I just know I'm feeling increasingly uneasy about briefings and our intelligence apparatus in general. It seems that with each passing day, more information flows out of the White House than flows into it. And lately, I'm feeling uneasy about the information that does come in. That all has to change!"

"So noted," Cornwall responded. "But why are we out here right now?"

"Because," the president explained, "I don't want this conversation on tape. For the time being, when someone tells me they will do something with intel I've seen, or I tell them to do something with it, I need you to quickly and quietly follow up on it to ensure it happens and that a minimum of hands, eyes, and ears are involved."

"Understood, Mr. President," Cornwall replied. "I do that most of the time already."

"You do, Jasper," the president agreed. "And you do it flawlessly when asked. Now I'm asking you to do it wall-to-wall. As I said, it's only for the time being—at least until we know we've got a handle on exactly who shares, studies, and safeguards classified material in the White House, and precisely how and when they do it. I know it'll consume a great deal of your time," the president said. "But it's vital, and it starts now."

"Consider it done," Cornwall said. "But can you at least tell me what prompted this?"

"It wasn't a particular event," the president replied. "It's an accumulation of things that have occurred, especially over the past two years. Chief among them are leaks that have had adverse impacts on a number of covert operations. Some were military, some were paramilitary, but each of them posed life or death risks to Americans and allies. And the leaks threatened their success. So we must do everything within our power to stop the damned leaks!"

"And I haven't known about any of this until now?"

Cornwall asked with irritation. "The leaks had to involve staff, of which I am your chief. It may have helped if I'd been advised about such events when they occurred. With all due respect, Mr. President, this assignment would likely be easier—perhaps even unnecessary—if you had kept me in the loop in the first place."

"Perhaps you're right—concerning the leaks," the president conceded. "But even more important, I'm growing increasingly concerned about the intel that is—and isn't —coming in."

"You're going to have to be a little more specific," Cornwall said.

"Take the matter of Captain Baird's removal from command of the Reagan, as just one example," the president began. "Do you know the details of why he was removed?"

"I don't," Cornwall replied.

"But you brought the related chapter from the Book to the Oval, when I allowed the captain to see some of the information, remember?" the president prompted him.

"Of course I remember," Cornwall shot back, "but I didn't read the material. I went to the vault off the Situation Room, where the Book is kept. Then I had the chapter you asked for retrieved, and I brought it directly to the Oval, as you requested."

"So you're saying that during your walk and elevator

ride from the Situation Room, you had more than 1,000 pages of information so secret it's confined to the Book, and you didn't so much as look at a single page?" the president asked to make his point.

"I did not," Cornwall replied flatly. "I'm confident that if you feel I should see information that's discussed in the Oval, you'll tell me to look it over. Otherwise, I don't."

"I know that, Jasper," the president said with a smile. "That's one of the million or so reasons you're my chief of staff. But I refuse to believe that none of the three we were briefed by yesterday morning knew at least some of the information that's in that chapter. Yet, they played dumb when Kramer asked me about it."

"You actually believe that one or more of them knows why and how Captain Baird was hustled off the *Ronald Reagan* in the middle of the Sea of Japan when not one of the *Reagan's* 6,000 crewmembers claims to have seen it happen?" Cornwall asked in astonishment.

"I do," the president answered. "For starters, a sonar operator was taken off the *Reagan* as well as Baird, precisely because he saw members of the team that evacuated them both. Then there's nearly the entire crew of the sub that escorted the Reagan back to Yoko-suka, Japan … along with Baird and the sonar operator and the team that brought them both aboard."

"And that's all in the Book?" Cornwall asked, but knew the answer.

"It's all there," the president replied flatly. "Not to hide the details surrounding the mission, but to safeguard the means by which it was accomplished. The weapons and tactics used in that operation will not likely ever be used like that again. But if they ever must be, we want to be sure the subject or subjects don't have any idea how it's done."

"So members of our intelligence agencies know what's in the Book of Secrets!" Cornwall stated the obvious while his brain was still processing it.

"None of them knows everything," President Prescott assured him. "But unfortunately, it's safe to assume that the heads of all 17 of our intelligence agencies each know some part of it. That shouldn't be too surprising," the president continued. "After all, a number of eyes review and select the information that I ultimately consider for inclusion in the Book. If I approve it, it gets keyed into Pinnacle as a new entry. Then someone else prints those details and adds them to the hard copy version. Others maintain and secure the hard copy. Still, others retrieve portions for review in the Situation Room, or here in the Oval. Then, of course, they replace them into the Book when they are returned.

"It takes countless staffers to make sure it all happens 'round the clock, 365 days a year. How many? I have no idea. How many of them know members of our intelligence community? I have no idea. How many are secretly being paid by one or more of those intelligence agencies? I have no idea."

"I never gave it much thought," Cornwall said.

"I often give it much thought," the president said softly. "The only part of this that's at all comical is what we paid for Pinnacle to keep our most important secrets secret."

"What's Pinnacle?" Cornwell couldn't resist asking.

"It's a massive freestanding, encrypted server," the president said with a shake of his head. "There are actually two side by side, each continually backing the other up to supposedly ensure the Book is completely secure, while it's also available to me—and you—24/7."

"So, it's not networked at all?" Jasper concluded.

"Nope!" the president confirmed. "No hacking or other unauthorized access is possible. They tell me only five people, one on each shift and two who are on-call as backups, know the access code—and they all must be present and participate in changing the code on a classified schedule that they jointly create and share with no one else. Sound secure enough to you?"

"It does!" Cornwall said with certainty.

"Yet I'm sure something's amiss in the system," the president said and looked across the south lawn at the White House. "Our best experts will tell you we work in the most secure location in the world, Jasper. And I believe them. But after thinking about all this night and day for weeks, I've come to an unhappy conclusion. With apologies to Shakespeare, something is rotten in the District of Columbia—and it's leaking. No pun intended.

"We better get back before the Secret Service rounds us up," the president said half in jest.

"I'm surprised they haven't already," Cornwall replied, silently grateful to soon be able to change into a pair of dry socks.

"Call Doc when you can," the note from Camilla on The Resolute Desk said.

"Camilla, please put me through to Doc," the president said into the intercom.

"I have Doc on the line, Mr. President," she said moments later.

"Good morning, Doc!" the president boomed into the phone. "It's good to hear your voice! Did you call for business or pleasure? Pleasure, I hope!"

"Business, I'm afraid, Mr. President," Doc answered. "Do you remember Thomas and Raymon Byrnes being at a thank-you luncheon you threw for my team a couple of years ago?"

"Sure, Doc," the president replied. "The FBI special agent and the Maricopa County Deputy Sheriff. How are they doing?"

"They're just fine, Mr. President," Doc replied. "And I believe they've stumbled onto something important I think you should hear about and see for yourself."

"Have they run it through their official channels already?" the president asked.

"They have," Doc said. "But no alarms went off, and I think this may be too important to wait until their official channels wake up and smell the coffee, if you know what I mean."

"Well, Lord knows I've learned to trust your instincts, Doc," the president said. "I can have my 757 waiting for you at Glacier International at 0600 tomorrow. That'll get you into Andrews by early afternoon. Keep things short and sweet here, and you just might get back to Montana in time for supper, which should make it easier to get Connie's buy-in. Sound good?"

"I'll make it work at my end, Mr. President," Doc said. "Thanks for making time for this."

"Thanks for all you and the team do, Doc," the president replied. "Will Q be with you?"

"I doubt I could keep him away," Doc laughed. "But, you know he'll expect lunch."

"No problem there," the president chuckled. "But I doubt I'll be able to join you. So you'll probably be joined by the vice president or Jasper."

"S'okay by me," Doc said. "I haven't had any time with either of them in a while. I'm sure you're quite busy, and I gotta let Connie know. I'll talk to you tomorrow, Mr. President."

"Looking forward to it!" the president boomed and ended the call.

Just about the time Doc entered the lake house to break the news of his trip to Connie, Jasper stepped out of the West Wing elevator and into the Situation Room. The American public still thought of it as a simple 5,525-square-foot room, officially dubbed the John F. Kennedy Conference Room, holding little more than one long conference table and some wall-mounted flat screens that sit idle most of the time, waiting for a domestic or foreign "situation" to arise. But it had long been transformed into a circular, 50,000-square-foot high-tech mecca of bustling activity, where dozens of analysts and military experts monitor and assess audio, visual, and digital information acquired from human, electronic, and satellite sources around the clock.

"Hello, Mr. Cornwall!" Navy Corporal Chance Oliver, the Situation Room director, called out to him from the catwalk that encircled the room ten feet above the floor. "What's up?" he asked as he descended the steel spiral staircase to greet Cornwall face-to-face.

Cornwall had met with Chance on a number of occasions, but he still was not used to the fact that such a youthful, fresh-faced "kid" just 27 years old had the knowledge, experience, and poise to run the Situation Room as effectively as he did. Chance silently led his visitor into a small soundproof room off the Situation Room, locked the door, and switched on ambient music to drown out their conversation.

"What brings you down among us basement dwellers this time?" Chance asked with a grin.

"Just following up on the president's directive that 18 satellite images of Chinese nuclear Jin-class subs shown to him during yesterday's Daily Briefing got uploaded to Pinnacle," Cornwall told him.

"The Chinese sub-images are the most amazing I've seen yet!" Chance said. "Have you seen them?"

"I have," Cornwall responded. "Now, I need to confirm they're in the system."

"Uploaded and secured!" Chance said tersely. "And I can hardly believe how incredibly clear they are."

"They're digital images, taken from low earth orbit, correct?" Cornwall asked.

"Yes, but the LEO was the maximum 1,200 miles," Chance said. "Yet they are the clearest and sharpest I've ever seen. President Prescott must have been surprised to learn that China has at least twice as many Jin-class subs as we thought. We certainly were."

"You didn't have a clue?" Cornwall asked because the president would want to know.

"Not one," Chance shot back emphatically. "But to be clear, China originally announced its intention to build a total of eight 094As when they acknowledged having the first one in 2007. We never expected 12. So we had a lot of questions the minute we saw the images yesterday.

Questions like: How did China manage to secretly build a half-dozen more of its largest class of nuclear subs and arm each of them with a dozen JL-3 MIRVs? Where exactly did the Chinese build the additional subs? Did they build them inside that mountain we thought was only a base? Are they building more? If so, how are they doing it? How do they sneak in the volume of materials and supplies required for such a massive project? Is the mountain's interior also home to the thousands of workers a program that size requires?"

"That's quite a list of vitally important questions, Corporal," Cornwall noted.

"Oh, the list is even longer—and still growing—believe me," Chance said. "Meanwhile, there's a lot about this discovery that makes no sense," Chance finally said.

"Go on," Cornwall encouraged him. "I'm all ears."

"The primary role of any nation's nuclear sub fleet is as a deterrent to first strikes," Chance explained. "Nations that might consider a first-strike nuclear attack on an enemy possessing a fleet of atomic subs armed with nuclear warheads can never be absolutely sure of the locations of those subs and their rockets. Such devastating weapons, so mobile and elusive, help ensure a target nation can launch one or more retaliatory strikes.

"So it's curious that China would tip its hand by clustering its nuclear sub fleet that way, especially at the Yulin Navy Base, which they refuse to acknowledge even exists," Chance noted. "The Chinese Navy is craftier than that. It's a needless, counterproductive show of strength. They know we, and several other nations, routinely monitor the entrance to the underground base. Putting the subs on display there not only disclosed the size of their fleet, it gave us time to reposition our pacific hydrophones and LEO satellites to track each of them as they redeploy. If they wanted that to happen, why build them in secret?"

"Those questions are all quite intriguing, Corporal," Cornwall said with a sigh. "It could be critical to the nation for the president to have the answers."

"That's why we're here, sir," Chance said with a smile. "Our mission is to have the answers to intriguing questions when the president needs them."

"On that note, the president has a meeting with the Joint Chiefs scheduled for early next week," Cornwall said. "But I've got a feeling he'll move it up to tomorrow when I relay your thoughts and questions to him. Sorry if that adds pressure to the situation."

"No problem!" Chance said with a smile and a shrug. "Situation normal!"

4

RETURN OF THE GUARDIANS

As Cornwall wrapped up his conversation with Corporal Oliver in the Situation Room, Doc headed to the kitchen of the lake house to give Connie the news that he and Q were taking the Byrnes brothers to D.C. the next morning. As the retired Navy SEAL and Secret Service agent stepped into the large, naturally lighted gourmet kitchen that Connie had always wanted, he caught sight of Thomas and Raymon Byrnes in two of Connie's frilliest aprons and collapsed against the huge side by side refrigerator in wild laughter.

"Did you two lose a bet or something?" Doc said when he caught his breath.

"We can't possibly look that funny," Raymon answered him curtly.

"Wanna bet?" Doc shot back and laughed again. "Oh, wait. You've already lost a bet."

"We didn't lose a bet, Doc!" Raymon said in mild frustration. "We're just helping this terrific wife of yours whip up one of her legendary suppers for tonight."

"Don't upset these two, John," Connie told her husband. "Good help is hard to find."

"You're working on supper already?" Doc asked in surprise. "What's the rush?"

"There's no rush, my dear," Connie told him. "Tomorrow is Jenny's birthday, and I've invited everyone over to celebrate it with her favorite meal tonight. So I got an early start."

"What are we having, and why are we having it tonight?" Doc asked predictably.

"We're making her favorite, a corn bread-stuffed turkey with all the trimmings: sweet potatoes, mashed potatoes, gravy, green beans, corn, dinner rolls, cranberries, and pumpkin pie with my signature homemade whipped cream," Connie said with pride. "And we're having it tonight because I've heard you and the rest of the team may not be home tomorrow night."

"Who would dare start such a rumor?" Doc replied with mock displeasure. "I've told no one any such thing."

"You didn't have to, John darling," Connie said in resignation. "I could read the writing on the wall when Tom and Ray told me you were calling the president about Mancini, the ring, and the Guardians. So what time do you plan to leave tomorrow?"

"Around 0500," Doc answered, relieved that Connie was already on the same page regarding the trip. "The president's sending his personal 757 tonight, and we'll take off for D.C. at 0600. If all goes well, we'll be home by suppertime."

"While you're gone, I'll pack your duffle bag in case I'm right," Connie told him.

"What's that supposed to mean?" Doc asked. "Are you throwing me out?"

"That's not funny, John!" Connie said. "I just know you, and if your meeting with the president leads you to believe you and the team can help eradicate the Guardians once and for all, you'll be here just long enough to grab a bag and kiss me goodbye 'til the job is done."

"And Q tells me I get the cart out in front of the horse!" Doc chuckled. "I'm just going to talk this through with the president. And Q and the Byrnes brothers are simply coming along to answer questions the president may have. Honest!"

"One of the things I've learned about this line of work you and the team are in, John, is that you can seldom predict where you'll head next—and when you'll be back. But don't worry. I know why you do it … and I love you for it. Just promise me you'll be careful."

"I'm always careful, Beauty," Doc told her softly as he pulled her close. "You know that.

"The only risk I've ever taken was asking you out for our first time. And look how that has worked out!"

"I'm being serious, John," Connie said curtly. "Don't treat me like I'm not smart enough to know the risks you and the team take on these missions. Have you forgotten that Marsha and I have been in the thick of things with the team a couple of times? Just come home to me safe and sound. Okay?"

"Okay," Doc said simply and pulled his wife even closer and kissed her deeply right in the middle of the kitchen, with the Byrnes brothers looking on.

"Now that's what true love looks like," Thomas told his brother and lightly jabbed an elbow into his ribs. "You need to find the right girl like I did and get you some of that."

"Mind your own business, Tom," Raymon said in genuine irritation. "I get plenty."

"If you say so, Brother," Thomas chuckled. "But you're always grumpy for a reason."

"I'd better call Q and fill him in about tomorrow," Doc said as he looked at the brothers again and laughed some more as he pulled his cell phone from his back pocket.

"No pictures!" Thomas yelled and pulled off his apron even faster than his brother.

"Boys! You don't trust me!" Doc chuckled in mock

offense. "I'd never take your pictures without your consent. Not while you're both looking at me."

Doc stepped outside onto the large deck that overlooked Montana's majestic Flathead Lake. He speed-dialed Q while he took in the breathtaking sight of Thunderbolt Mountain towering over Flathead National Forest just across the crystal clear water.

"Hey, Doc!" Q's voice jumped from the phone. "To what do I owe this honor? Do you need Marsha and me to bring a dish to tonight's supper? I make a mean grilled cheese. Do you prefer American cheese or Swiss, wheat bread or rye?"

"Q! … Are you done?" Doc said impatiently. "I need to talk to you about something."

"Man, oh man," Q sighed. "Lighten up, Doc. It's only a little past 10:00 a.m., and you're wound up tighter than a cheap watch. You're healthy, married to a wonderful woman, and wealthier than you ever dreamed. And all while you're still relatively young."

"Q! Stop!" Doc almost shouted. "I'm taking the Byrnes brothers to meet with the president, and I need you along."

"No problem, Doc. You know that. Anytime, anywhere, always," Q said seriously. "I'm assuming this is about the Guardians and that Mancini character. Am I right?"

"Exactly," Doc said. "We need to shake the trees on this

one, and since we can shake at the very top, we need to do that."

"What time are we leaving?" Q asked.

"We need to be aboard the president's 757 at Glacier Park when it takes off at 0600," Doc told him.

"So, I'll be down to your place by 0500, okay?" Q proposed.

"That'll work," Doc said. "Thanks, Q. I know it's short notice."

"Anytime, anywhere, always," Q said again. "But I have to go now. I'm helping Marcia hang curtains. See you in a few hours for supper. We can talk more then."

"Roger that," Doc said and ended the call.

He wasn't surprised when Q and Marsha were the first to arrive that afternoon. Madeleine and Noah knocked on the front door just minutes later with their arms full of presents for Jenny.

"I've talked to you two several times now about not needing to knock," Connie chided them playfully. "Our house is your house. But don't worry, there's no mortgage. Kick off your shoes and get comfortable. You're going to be here a while."

Before Noah and Madeleine picked out easy chairs near the fireplace in the den, Jenny and Louis were at the door. Connie let them in on her way to the den, carrying three bottles of chilled wine. Thomas followed close behind with a large tray full of wine glasses, and Raymon was close behind him with a tray of cheese, fruit, and crackers.

"Excuse my bare feet," Connie told the crowd, "but I've got a half-hour before I need to be back in the kitchen, and I figured I would give everyone a wine-drinking lesson."

Two hours later, supper wound down, and the conversation picked up.

"Well, birthday girl," Connie said to Jenny. "Q and Marsha's house is finally finished, and work is almost complete on Noah and Madeleine's place. So I'm wondering if you two have made up your minds about whether or not you're going to settle down here too."

"We do love it here," Jenny replied. "And President Prescott has assured us that we're assigned to provide you all protection indefinitely. So Louis and I have been talking seriously about buying the place we're renting. It's nothing as fancy as this, but we can afford it, and we love Rollins. So it seems like a good investment."

"And Rollins makes for a better return address than Poison on your stationery," Q added.

"Don't knock Poison," Doc said. "It's a nice, peaceful town."

"Sure it is," Q chuckled. "With a name like that, not many people visit, let alone stay."

"The president has designated the two of you our protectors," Doc said with a sly smile to change the subject. "Having seen you both in action, I must say that I feel quite safe."

"After that wild episode on your front lawn with the Guardians a while back, I'm not at all sure who's protecting who," Louis said. "And if the Guardians are alive and well like you theorized last night, Madeleine, we may all need to watch each other's backs a while longer."

"Speaking of your theory, Madeleine, it would be helpful if you can go to the White House with me and Q and Tom and Ray and tell the president what you told us," Doc said hopefully. "We've got the use of the president's personal jetliner, so we'll be home for supper."

"Well," Madeleine began with a glance Noah's way, "if you don't have anything planned for tomorrow, we can both go. What do you think, babe?"

"Sounds good to me," Noah said. "Count us in."

"Count us in too!" Jenny said as she grabbed Louis's hand. "You said I could pick the place where we would celebrate my birthday. I pick the White House! I hope Melania's there!"

"What time do we leave?" Louis asked with a smile.

"Be here by 0500 hours," Doc said flatly.

"Guess we'd better have dessert and head home to pack and get some sleep," Jenny said.

"We don't have a mission to discuss," Doc noted. "So you can nap during the flight."

"I doubt I'll need it," Jenny gushed. "A White House visit is still a very big deal to me."

"Well, Marsha," Connie chimed in, "looks like you and I will have the entire day to ourselves tomorrow. What do you say we spend it spending money in Missoula? I can call first thing in the morning and book a couple hours in that spa we enjoyed last month. That should get us in the mood to shop."

"I'm all in!" Marsha said with a broad smile.

"Hanging out with you costs me a lot of money, Doc," Q chuckled as he put an arm around Marsha's shoulders.

"Don't complain one bit, Quinton," Marsha prompted him. "Hanging out with Doc, as you put it, has made us more money than I can ever spend."

"For once, I hope you're right," Q replied and chuckled some more.

Everyone then pitched in to clear the table, load both dishwashers, put away the leftovers, and called it a night

"What terrific friends we have!" Connie said as she squeezed Doc and kissed him.

"Indeed!" Doc agreed. "And how terrific it will be when the missions end, and we can all stop worrying about each other's safety and just enjoy our lives together."

"Be sure to tell the president that tomorrow," Connie said and kissed him again. "Now take me to bed, and I'll do my best to let you get some sleep, my hero."

As usual, the president had two SUVs waiting for the team at Joint Base Andrews when the team arrived shortly after noon the next day. Doc inexplicably felt a need for high readiness the moment the plane touched down. So he had the team turn their covert earpieces on and set at low volume. He and Q were surprised to see uniformed Marine drivers waiting for them instead of the usual Secret Service contingent. But it didn't seem like that big of a deal at the time.

"Welcome, everyone!" the major driving the lead vehicle called out to the team as they stepped onto the tarmac. "President Prescott sends his regrets that he will not be able to join you for lunch. He and Vice President Kelly are both in a meeting for at least another two hours."

"Must be very important to last so long," Doc said as the vehicles headed to the White House.

"I'm sure it is, Doc," the major replied over his shoulder. "It's good to see you again, by the way."

"You too, Major Cooper," Doc replied with a weary smile. "But I'd be lying if I said I wanted to make this trip more often."

"I understand completely, Doc," the major replied as he drove the SUV through the D.C. traffic. "Is this trip for business or pleasure, or both?"

"Business only, this trip," Doc answered. "We hope to be on our way back to Montana by 1500 hours. So be sure to have these buggies ready to go at that time, if not sooner."

"Roger that!" the major shot back as he drove the gleaming black Suburban north on 15th Street toward the White House.

Doc was surprised when the major didn't turn west on E Street, the usual approach they took to access the White House via the North Gate at 17th Street and Pennsylvania Avenue.

"Construction's got both 17th and Pennsylvania blocked just west of the gate," the major explained as he continued up 15th to I Street. "We'll take I Street west, then take 17th south to the gate. It's just a little out of the way and shouldn't take us any longer. Sorry, Doc."

"No problem, Major," Doc replied. "Everything happens for a reason."

As the big SUV cruised west on I Street, Doc asked the major to change the plan and turn south on 16th Street instead of 17th so he could get a quick look at St. John's Episcopal Church, where the bizarre war with Jonah Baird and his Guardians began.

"Slow down when you get to St. John's, please, Major,

then circle the block, and you can resume your original plan to access the White House via 17th Street," Doc said.

"Roger that!" Major Cooper replied crisply and eased up on the gas pedal.

When they reached the church, Doc focused his attention on the building, and his mind flooded with memories of all that had happened there: memories of the small library hidden behind the altar. The library was where he used his SEAL trident to unlock the secret door that led to a mysterious chamber beneath the church where he first met with the Keeper. Doc recalled not having a clue during that first encounter that he and the Keeper would soon be at war with one another. It pained him to still be haunted by the possibility that the war might not yet be over.

Madeleine rode in the second vehicle and had no interest in the historic church. So she casually eyed the vehicles parked on the curb around it. As they headed east on 16th Street, she suddenly caught sight of two people sitting in a cargo van parked in front of the side entrance to the church. It shocked her to see them wearing bright, bold Juggalo makeup and black hoodies like the characters in her recent dream.

"Stop the car!" she told the driver urgently.

"Pausing!" the sergeant behind the wheel barked into his headset to Major Cooper in the lead vehicle and hit the brakes.

Madeleine suddenly thought better of having the SUV conspicuously idling in the middle of the street. She needed a low-profile position from which to watch what the suspicious pair in Juggalo makeup might do next. So she had the sergeant park the Suburban on the opposite side of the one-way street. Fortunately, there was enough room for the lead vehicle to pull in too.

"What's up?" Doc's said into the compact headsets the team members had with them.

"Just a hunch," Madeleine said calmly as she, Jenny, Noah, and Louis inserted their earpieces. "I spotted two individuals wearing Juggalo makeup—and there may be more—in a white cargo van parked outside the side entrance to the church."

"What the hell is Juggalo makeup," Q shot back to her.

"It's the white-face makeup like the rock bands Kiss, and Insane Clown Posse wear," Madeleine explained. "Don't laugh, but a few nights ago, I had a bad dream about people wearing makeup and hoodies like they're wearing. It gives me the creeps to see the real thing right in front of me, and I just have to sit here a few minutes to see if they're up to something."

"What's that about Juggalo makeup?" Major Cooper asked Doc.

"Madeleine spotted two people wearing it in that white cargo van parked beside the church," Doc told him. "It's made her suspicious, and she's just watching for their next move."

"They must be members of a band," Q chimed in. "What other possible reason could they have for wearing it in public in broad daylight?"

"Juggalo makeup thwarts facial recognition software," Thomas said from the rear seat. "And I doubt it's a coincidence that we're at one of the most monitored intersections in D.C. The church is smack in the middle of a historic district. And given all the protests that have been staged here over the past few weeks, there's a good chance there are more closed-circuit cameras within a hundred-yard radius of this intersection than just about anywhere else except Beijing. It appears that the pair don't want to be recognized. So it would be helpful to know who they are and why they might be parked outside the church."

"Maybe they're just a couple of protestors waiting for the right moment to picket the intersection or spray graffiti on the church," the sergeant driving the second SUV suggested. "But that activity has typically happened after dark. It's sure not a rock band. Not at midday during the week."

"Well, if they're not protestors or a rock band, what else can they be?" the major asked.

At precisely that moment, the Juggalo pair got out of the van, and six more who looked just like them exited its rear doors. They all wore black hoodies under long, black overcoats even though it was the middle of summer.

"They're all carrying something under their coats, and it looks like they're headed into the church," Madeleine said over the radio.

Doc and Q turned to each other in unison and said together, "They're Guardians!"

"There's eight of 'em," Q noted. "Looks like it'll be a fair fight."

"Don't be too sure of that, Q," Doc shot back. "More could be inside the church. Let 'em get inside before following them," Doc said. "I think they're headed to the basement. Don't move 'til I give the command. Take your safeties off, but don't draw your weapons unless and until you have to. Major Cooper, I think it wise for you and the sergeant to stay in your vehicles. No need to involve the military. That would result in way too much paperwork."

As Doc expected, the last Guardian out of the van paused at the church entrance and scanned the street to make sure they weren't being followed. He was quickly satisfied they hadn't been and joined the others inside. He was wrong.

"Move out!" Doc commanded. "Madeleine, lead your group in through the side door and wait for my instructions. I'm taking mine to the front."

"Hold this, please," Tom said to the major and handed

him the silver Guardian ring, then exited the Suburban with the rest of the team.

"What do you think they're up to?" Q asked Doc as they and the Byrnes brothers slowly walked up the broad front steps of the historic "Church of the Presidents." Their sidearms were ready but stayed under their light jackets.

"My guess is they're here on orders from that Mancini character, hoping to find cash Baird may have hidden in the secret basement area that served as his original Forbidden Library. I know what we'll do with them. But what will we do with any cash they find?"

"Interesting question, Q," Doc said. "But, it's above our paygrade."

"We don't have a paygrade!" Q noted for the record.

"I'm going in," Doc said into his radio. "Hold your positions."

He paused halfway through the entrance and counted a half-dozen people quietly seated or kneeling in various pews. There was no sign of the Guardians.

"Enter quietly, ten to fifteen seconds apart," he commanded. "No need to alarm anyone."

"Act like Episcopalians," Q said, to no one's surprise.

"Sit in separate pews and wait for my signal."

The eight scattered and spent five minutes in the pews they'd picked.

"When was the last time you were in church, Doc?" Madeleine asked to calm herself.

"When I buried a close friend, not far from here," Doc said sadly.

"Sorry to hear that," she replied softly.

"Don't be. He's in a far better place," Doc told her. "And it's an even better place because of it. I'm heading to the rear of the altar," he said to the team. "Follow my lead and enter the hidden door you'll see me open."

Moments later, the team stood around the pedestal Doc was surprised still stood at the center of the room with the large book still open upon it. The Guardians had left it turned to the trident-shaped hollow carved out of 100 or so of its center pages. Once again, Doc used his pocket knife to pry the trident from the grip of his cane, then he held a finger to his lips to signal silence as he placed the trident into the depression and a hidden door quietly slid open.

The team slipped through the door and descended to the basement without making a sound. Doc remembered the heavy, unlocked door at the bottom of the steps opened inward to the soundproof room where he first met Jonah Baird, who introduced himself as the "Keeper." The former SEAL nudged the door open just a quarter-inch and heard conversation in the room.

"There's at least a hundred rows of shelves in here, and we've checked 'em all," one Guardian told another. "Nothing's here!"

"Well, we'd better be damned sure of that before we even think of telling it to Lord Mancini. So keep looking!" the Guardian shouted. "Move the shelves! Check for hidden panels in the walls and floor! Lord Mancini was certain the Keeper hid gold and silver here. We must search until we find it!"

Doc carefully let the door close and whispered into his radio, "You were right, Madeleine. The ring's legit. Mancini is now pulling the Guardians' strings. Pick a stair and get comfortable, folks," he said. "Let's give them a little longer to search. Better them than us."

The team got as comfortable as possible in the darkened stairwell and waited.

"How long are we going to wait, Doc?" Q asked impatiently through the radio. "It's going to be mighty awkward if they come through that door and find us sitting on our hands."

"Take a deep breath, Q," Doc calmly whispered over the radio. "I'll give 'em just a few more minutes to search. Any amount of gold and silver worth hiding here has to be behind a panel too big to miss for very long."

Precisely ten minutes later, Doc cautiously nudged the door open again and heard the news.

"Found it!" a Guardian shouted. "There's at least 100 gold bars and 200 silver in here!"

Doc quickly did the math in his head and got wide-eyed. If the Guardian was close to right about the number of bars, he'd just found close to $80 million.

"Weapons ready!" Doc ordered by radio. "We're going in low! Tom, as FBI, you're in command!"

Doc kicked the heavy door open wide, dove into the room, and rolled to the right to make room for the seven who dove in behind him. All eight quickly rose to one knee in firing position.

"FBI! Drop your weapons, hands behind your heads, and freeze!" Thomas shouted, drew his Sig Sauer P228, and braced for a firestorm.

But the Juggalo-painted Guardians froze ... at first.

"You gotta warrant?" the bossy one shouted and began to slowly lower his arms.

Doc pointed his new Ruger Super Redhawk Alaskan Toklat .454 at the Guardian and held it rock-steady with both hands.

"Please don't make me use this," he said calmly. "It will nail you to the concrete wall behind you, and my shoulder will ache tonight."

"Go ahead and nail him, Doc," Q said sarcastically. "He probably deserves it."

Thomas prepared to fire his P228 in the line of duty for the very first time.

"No one has to get hurt!" he announced. "Do as I say, and we'll spare each other a lot of pain and suffering. Keep your hands behind your heads and kneel on the floor. Now!"

But the Guardians stood their ground in a nerve-wracking staring match.

Q pulled his jacket open to expose his U.S. Marshal badge and drew his second 40 caliber Smith & Wesson M&P from under it. Aiming both of them confidently, he said, "I swear, if y'all don't follow the man's instructions, I'm going to use both of these on every last one of you."

"You can't just shoot us!" a Guardian shouted.

"If you believe that, step out in front of the crowd," Q said like he meant it.

Doc hoped that would bring the standoff to an end. But it didn't. A Guardian at the rear of the bunch moved a little too fast for Raymon's comfort, and the next thing everybody heard was the chilling sound of the deputy pulling the hammer back on his Colt Anaconda .44 Magnum.

"One more move," he grunted. "Just one more move, and I'm all in."

The Guardian who moved fired a .45 Bond Arms Snake

Slayer derringer he had hidden in his hood. In that instant, the bossy one in the front of the bunch, whose eyes were fixed on Doc, reached back into his hood, and Q blasted him with both of his 40 calibers. The Guardian fell to the floor dead silent, and a seven-inch Thunderbolt throwing knife tumbled out of his hood.

"Freeze!" Thomas shouted, hoping the Guardians had had enough.

As he shouted, a bullet grazed his rib cage. He stumbled back a step but instinctively returned fire and put a round into the heart of the shooter, killing him instantly. Then he fired a second round into the Guardian he'd just killed, hoping the sight would make his point with the Guardians who were still alive and the massacre would end.

"Freeze damn it!" he shouted with his heart pounding. "Enough of this shit! You're all either going to give it up here and now—or die here in a moment! Which will it be?"

The remaining Guardians fell to their knees with their hands behind their heads and let Raymon bind them with Cobra zip cuffs he had in the thigh pockets of his cargo pants.

"Do you always have those on you?" Doc asked in amazement.

"When we're on the job," Raymon said and led the Guardians up the stairs.

Doc was relieved to see that the pews were empty when his team emerged from the library at the rear of the altar and marched the Guardians out the side door of the church, where both SUVs were waiting. Doc had Major Cooper summon transport for the Guardians and a small contingent of Marines to secure the gold and silver in the basement.

"Where do you want these basement rats delivered?" the major asked.

"Good question," Doc replied. "I guess we'll ship 'em to the brig at Joint Base Andrews until we hear from the president. But make sure no one questions them just yet."

"Hey! Aren't we supposed to be at a lunch meeting right about now?" Q interrupted as only he could. "I'm starving. Shoot-outs always make me hungry. Let's get to the White House!"

5

THE SINGLE DEFINED OBJECTIVE

About that time, Cornwall walked briskly to keep up as the president headed to the Oval, trying desperately to tie up some loose ends before losing him indefinitely to the meeting with the Joint Chiefs.

"How soon are you hoping to meet with Captain Baird about the senior advisor post?" he asked while dodging the bustling foot traffic.

"This evening over supper, if he can make it," the president said.

"This evening?" Cornwall asked in astonishment. "Aren't you going to ask for input from the chiefs?"

"I'm going to run it by them, but my mind's made up," the president stated flatly.

"Be gentle, Mr. President," Cornwall said softly.

"Remember, you're still hoping for the unanimous support for re-election."

"I've given them everything they've asked me for so far," the president said with a wink. "They'll give me this one without a fight."

"I hope you're right," Cornwall sighed. "What about the China situation? Do you want a statement to the media prepared? Will it include the chiefs' reactions and recommendations?"

"We're going to keep a lid on that one as long as possible, Jasper," the president said. "I want my feet under me when the questions start flying, and I'm not nearly there yet. "Is that it?"

"Anything you want me to relay to Holiday and his team during my meeting with them?"

"Tell 'em I hope to see them soon," the president said over his shoulder with a smile as he rushed into the Oval. "And tell 'em to be sure they're registered to vote in November."

"But they're not all citizens ..." Cornwall said before realizing the president knew it.

Camilla spotted Cornwall as he shuffled through pages in a file folder.

"Doc and his crew just arrived, Jasper," she told him. "Should I have them brought to the Map Room, or have you made other arrangements for your luncheon meeting?"

"The Map Room and a deli buffet is ready and waiting for us, Camilla," Cornwall told her. "Thanks for double-checking. Doc says they have something important to discuss. So hold my calls, please ... unless, of course, Mrs. Cornwall calls. I'll never make that mistake again. I expect my meeting will end long before the president is done pressing the Chiefs. So I'll be in the Situation Room until the President is available again. Please call me when he is."

"Will do, Jasper," Camilla cheerfully said. "Be careful with your tie during lunch."

"I will," Cornwall chuckled. "That's another mistake I won't make again."

Doc and his team were checking out the buffet they found waiting for them when Cornwall joined them in the Map Room.

"Hello!" he boomed in his best President Prescott impression. "It's been a while. How in the world have you all been? Please introduce me to your newest members, Doc."

"Presidential Chief of Staff Jasper Cornwall, I'd like you to meet Maricopa Sheriff's Deputy Commander Raymon Byrnes and his brother, FBI Special Agent Thomas Byrnes," Doc said proudly. "These two are the reason we're here this afternoon. As a matter of fact, they also gave us our first tip that Jonah Baird was masterminding a global murder campaign."

"I know of that," Cornwall said and shook their hands enthusiastically. "The President has spoken highly of you both. And he's given me official letters of appreciation for your service to the nation signed by him for both of you. I'll have them for you when you leave today."

The Byrnes brothers high-fived each other, and Doc and the team applauded.

"Let's eat!" Q shouted and rubbed his hands together.

"By all means!" Cornwall said and motioned for Thomas and Raymon to lead the way.

Once the meal was underway, Cornwall asked, "So what valuable information have you uncovered this time?"

"We took this ring off a suspected Guardian and bank robber in Phoenix a little more than a week ago," Thomas said and handed the ring across the table to Cornwall. " The 'L. Mancini' engraved in it belongs to Lorenzo Mancini, whom we believe murdered Culver Ainsley in Rome three years ago as part of Jonah Baird's effort to build his Forbidden Library. It appears he's assumed command of the Guardians since Baird's death … and that he's even more maniacal."

"That's a chilling development," Cornwall said. "How sure are you of all this?"

"It was just a theory when we arrived here today," Doc

told him. "But we just confirmed it in a confrontation with a band of Guardians at St. John's Church."

"You just confronted Guardians right across the street from here?" Cornwall asked in amazement. "How bad was it?"

"Shots were fired, I'm afraid," Doc replied quietly.

"Casualties?" Cornwall asked hesitantly.

"Two—both were Guardians," Doc said. "Thomas has a flesh wound. But he's tough enough to heal."

"Are you sure you're alright?" Cornwall excitedly asked Thomas.

"I bandaged it in the Suburban. It's not even bleeding now," Thomas assured him.

"Still, we'll have the White House medical team clean and dress it when we're done here," Cornwall said. "I assume there were more than two Guardians. Where are they now?"

"Major Cooper arranged their transport to Joint Base Andrews," Doc said. "I figured that's the best place for them until the president decides what to do with 'em."

"Send 'em to Gitmo like you did with Baird," Q piped-up. "But don't let them escape."

"That's not funny, Q," Doc blurted out.

"It's just a suggestion," Q said. "A pretty good one too."

"What were they doing at St. John's?" Cornwall asked.

"Well, Baird somehow commandeered basement space there for his original Forbidden Library," Doc reminded him. "Mancini sent a squad there to look for loot he thought Baird may have secretly kept there. He was right too. They found gold and silver bars stashed in a large, very well-hidden wall safe. I took photos of them with my phone. Best I can tell, their value is north of $75 million. So I hope Major Cooper puts his best men on guard duty until the president decides what to do with the bars."

"Really?" Cornwall asked rhetorically. "It'll be nice to give the president the good news."

"I'd say it more than pays for our lunch," Q quipped. "Please tell President Prescott he can simply sign my letter of appreciation with, 'The Prez.'"

"You're impossible," Doc chided his friend and brother-in-arms.

"It's great bein' me, Doc," Q beamed. "It truly is!"

"So how do you propose we stop the Guardians once and for all?" Cornwall asked.

"I'm not sure," Doc sighed. "And to tell you the truth, it's now well outside our original mission. When Baird was a specter of international evil and untold power, his capture was our mission. But he's dead now, and Guardian activities are outside our parameters. My team and I can't very well chase them around the country, in and out of one jurisdiction after another, from coast to coast and back again. So we humbly hand them off to the FBI and NSA."

"I understand your point, Doc," Cornwall conceded. "I know the president would like to retain your services through to the end. But frankly, my counsel to him will be that it would be a very risky legal strategy ... and quite frankly, an even riskier political strategy should something go wrong in the heat of his re-election campaign."

"BINGO!" Q blurted out. "That's the clincher. Our job is done!"

"Now, just a moment," Cornwall said forcefully. "Your service to the nation, though practically thankless, will always be needed. The unique circumstances that shaped your involvement with Jonah Baird and his international band of Guardians may, indeed, have expired. But the president has no other resource that's your equal. And he will no doubt want to be able to rely upon your services if circumstances call for them ... whether it happens late in his second term or early next week. I sincerely hope none of you will walk away from that role lightly."

"Make no mistake," Doc replied. "We take great pride in our usefulness to the nation. We've never taken it lightly. But you yourself cited the complexities and unique circumstances that must align for us to be activated rather than the formal investigative and law enforcement agencies under the president's command.

My team and I have never taken our role lightly. But it can take a heavy toll. By the grace of God, I haven't lost a single member of this team in the line of duty. And I intend to do my best to keep it that way.

"I came here today determined to impress that upon the president. We'll never shrink from a call to duty. But Baird's removal from the equation was the single defined objective our team had. I concede to you and to the team that at times my enthusiasm overrode my judgment and resulted in greater involvement than was wise —and safe—for the team and for the president's political future."

"I hear what you're saying, Doc," Cornwall replied. "I've scanned the Book thoroughly, and I'm convinced your team is the greatest that never existed in our nation's history."

"The Book?" Doc asked with a squint.

"The Book," Cornwall repeated himself with a wry grin. "Euphemistically referred to as the 'President's Book of Secrets.'"

"That really exists?" Madeleine couldn't restrain herself from asking.

"Unlike what most people probably imagine," Cornwall said simply. "As a whole, it's comprised of countless pages of historical transcripts, facts, images, thoughts, and theories which could never be bound into a single book. But as you can imagine, our intelligence agencies gather new transcripts, facts, images, thoughts, theories, and other information every day, and deliver them to the president and a few select members of his administration in a Daily Presidential Briefing, uploaded to iPads around here simply called the 'Book.' When a briefing is concluded, the contents of the Book are added to the presidential archive, dramatically nicknamed the 'President's Book of Secrets.'"

"Well, I can strike that off my list of Grand Mysteries," Madeleine sighed.

"I guess this concludes our meeting," Cornwall announced. "I thank you sincerely for coming and for bringing us the valuable information about the Guardians … and for corralling a few of them while you were at it. Special Agent Byrnes, I'll call down to Major Cooper right now and make sure he provides you with an affidavit of transfer for the ring. Then I'll get it over to the evidence analysis lab at the J. Edger building this afternoon. Thank you all again!"

"Thank YOU!" Thomas bellowed with a sigh of relief and a feeling of accomplishment.

"Goodbye!" the team practically cheered as they headed to get Thomas bandaged, then headed out the north portico, where the SUVs were waiting to take them back to Joint Base Andrews for their flight home.

"With a good tailwind, we just might be home for supper," Doc said, looking at his watch.

6

The president was typically positive—effusive even. It came naturally to him. But the truth was, he had to fake it mightily as he welcomed his Joint Chiefs of Staff to the small conference room off the Oval that afternoon. For a brief moment, he wished he was eating hard salami and Swiss cheese between two thick slices of dark, whole-grain bread and washing it down with an icy Diet Coke while enjoying the company of Doc and the rest of the President's Dozen. But he quickly snapped out of it and got down to business with the eight most powerful, most influential members of his administration, besides himself, of course.

As he took his seat, he quietly pondered why, despite all their power and influence, the chiefs still needed the affirmation supplied by a simple paper name tent where they sat at the table with him. He knew their names and ranks very well. But he focused on the bright side of the tents having been demanded. At least there was no chance he'd accidentally confuse their names or ranks during the meeting.

There they were, seated around the roundtable behind their name tents with what he'd dubbed "almost-smiles":

Chairman of the Joint Chiefs of Staff General Lawrence R. Luceous

Vice Chairman of the Chiefs of Staff General Martin S. Gallaway

Chief of Staff of the Army General Richard T. Cole

Chief of Staff of the Air Force General Elizabeth R. Rosenthal

Chief of Naval Operations Admiral Bryce Bridgewater

Commandant of the Marine Corps General Joseph E. Robinson

Chief of Space Operations General William H. Walker

Chief of the National Guard Bureau General Wanda T. Booker

No lunch at this meeting, the president thought as he heard his stomach growl. *Look at the bright side,* the President silently reminded himself, *the meeting will be over sooner!*

The president took notes while the chiefs talked through a litany of issues, plans, and needs. He knew the meeting was recorded. The chiefs knew it too. But ever since every one of them got their undershorts in a knot when he didn't take notes during their very first meeting with him, he made sure he had a pen and a notepad and used both when the chiefs spoke.

When they'd finished, he asked them some perfunctory questions and then finally got to the point of his having moved the meeting up by a week … which none of them asked about.

"I know you're all wondering why I moved this meeting up a week," the president began, "so I've had the Situation Room prepare a slide show for your review. Please follow me down there now, and I'll explain in detail once the presentation begins."

Corporal Oliver was ready and waiting for them beside a fifteen-foot screen emblazoned with:

V. A. S. E. VIEWS

(Vigilant All-Seeing Eye Reconnaissance Satellite # 133)

Type 094A Jin Class Nuclear Submarines

South China Sea / Yulin Naval Base

~ 1133 Hours / May 13 ~

"As you watch the presentation," the president told them, "remember that there's a lot we don't yet know about the warships captured in the following images by one of our reconnaissance satellites roughly 1,200 miles above the South China Sea last Thursday at approximately 1800 hours, D.C. time."

The president pressed his remote, and the first image appeared in stark, alarming detail.

"This, as you are all aware, is a photo of one of China's six known Type 094A Jin Class nuclear subs just a couple hundred yards off the coast of Hainan Island as it's approaching the mouth of the underground base China secretly dug beneath the island's tallest mountain over the past seven years," the president told them and pressed the remote again.

"In this photo, you see all six of the known 094As within a roughly one-mile radius as they sail away from the base. Now, as you also know, China publicly acknowledged its plans to build a total of eight of the subs, each fitted with 12 MIRVs, during its initial unveiling of the first of its Jin Class fleet nearly a decade ago. In the years since, we've seen five more in these same waters—and we have anticipated the additional two."

The president paused a moment for dramatic effect, then pressed the remote again.

"What we never anticipated was that we would someday capture this image containing no less than twelve of the deadly warships, each of which is equipped with enough megatonnage to obliterate several major cities in the contiguous 48 states."

A low, barely audible gasp emanated from somewhere across the table from the president's chair, and the president took it as his cue to move to the next slide, which showed the dozen deadly instruments of doom under greater magnification.

"I'm sure you're already processing the numerous implications of this revelation," the president told them. "I'm also confident that you have important questions for me, and I can assure you that I have some for you. So you go first."

"Am I correct in believing the DNI brought these images to your attention?" Army General Richard Cole asked.

"That's correct, General, together with CIA Director Reed and Commander Kramer of the Office of Naval Intelligence, during yesterday's Daily Briefing," the president said. "Of course, we're busily pursuing answers to the obvious questions: How did the Chinese manage to build these literally right under our noses? Are there more under that mountain and under construction? And so forth. And so on."

The president then quickly ushered them back to the Oval and announced, "I would appreciate receiving any and all additional questions in writing any time after this meeting. And I would especially appreciate your input regarding the real and potential implications of this development. If you have some now, let me hear them, please."

"For starters," General Cole began, "Yulin is located at the point in Chinese territory that is closest to the continental shelf. It's 150 nautical miles from the closest of the disputed Paracel Islands as well as the city of Da Nang, Vietnam. We believe the Chinese intend to expand Yulin to greatly increase the capabilities of their aircraft carrier groups."

"This could have significant economic as well as military impacts," Admiral Bridgewater added. "More than half of the world's annual merchant fleet tonnage passes through the Strait of Malacca, Sunda Strait, and Lombok Strait, with the majority continuing on into the South China Sea. Tanker traffic through the Strait of Malacca leading into the South China Sea is more than three times the annual Suez Canal traffic and well over five times more than the Panama Canal.

"China has claimed almost that entire body of water and is building numerous naval bases in the South China Sea to control them. A fleet of 094As this large adds a major threat in their bid for total control of the area," Bridgewater concluded.

"The fact that Yulin is only a few miles from the city of Sanya further complicates the strategic implications," General Rosenthal added. "Sanya's an extremely popular tourist destination and the site of a major planned cruise hub. Yulin's also adjacent to the Yalong Bay National Resort District and a great many resort hotels, all of which present made-to-order human shields and squelch any thoughts of military action to curb or counter China's continued expansion and domination in the region."

"With those insights, I conclude this meeting and repeat my request that you submit related questions, concerns, thoughts, and suggestions in writing to my office no later than a week from today, and I promise to provide you with my responses and reactions shortly thereafter.

"Oh, and one more thing. I plan to meet with retired Navy Captain Augustus Tucker Baird this evening to discuss the possibility of his joining my staff as Senior Advisor for Strategic Military Affairs," the president told them. "Of course, I value and invite your thoughts regarding the appointment. So I welcome your input and questions," the president told them.

"I think he's an excellent choice," Admiral Bridgewater said. "I served with Captain Baird in the Sea of Japan and found his knowledge and perceptions of potential enemies' tactics especially balanced and well-rounded, and his command style was receptive to input from junior officers, while also decisive when needed."

"You took the words right out of my mouth," Air Force General Rosenthal added. "I had the opportunity to watch his command style and tactics up close from one end of the South China Sea to the other for nearly three years, and I found both his tactical knowledge and command style exemplary. I believe he brings the right experience, knowledge, and skill set for the job."

"My thanks to both of you for your assessments of his knowledge, judgment, and qualifications," the president said as he got up from his desk to end the meeting and walked the chiefs to the door, where he dispensed enthusiastic handshakes.

The chiefs left him with a certainty that he'd identified the right person for the job. Fortunately, the captain was able to join the president for a dinner meeting that evening, and Major Cooper delivered him to the North

Portico shortly before 6:00 p.m. From there, a Marine lieutenant escorted him up the Grand Staircase to the First Family's private quarters on the second floor, to the First Family's intimate dining room, where a beautifully set table awaited him.

The lieutenant quickly departed, leaving the captain to take a close look at the paintings that hung there while he anxiously awaited the president's arrival.

"Good evening, Captain Baird!" the president's voice boomed the moment he entered the dining room. "Thank you for coming on such short notice. I greatly appreciate your availability, and I've asked the kitchen staff to do their best with prime rib this evening. I've been told it's your favorite. How are you, Captain?"

"It feels terrific to be invited here again so soon, Mr. President," the captain said. "Prime rib sounds wonderful. But please call me Tuck. I've been 'Tuck' to my friends all my life."

"So Tuck it shall be!" the president said. "Though you'll still be Captain Baird on the job."

"On the job?" Tuck asked in confusion. "I'm retired, Mr. President."

"Please have a seat, Tuck," the president said with a smile and sat directly across the table from him. "I invited you to supper, hoping that I might convince you to come out of retirement," the president confessed. "I very much need a rock-solid senior advisor for Strategic Military Affairs, and I'd appreciate it if you would agree to serve our nation in that capacity."

"Well, I'm flattered, of course, Mr. President," the captain said. "But I'm not at all sure I'm the best choice for such an important post."

"Of course you are, Tuck!" the president boomed as he pulled his chair closer to the table. "I've already run this by the Joint Chiefs, and they couldn't be happier about you as my pick to fill the job."

"Really?" Captain Baird blurted out. "Is that so?"

"That's so!" the president confirmed happily. "Two of them stated emphatically that you have the right experience, knowledge, and skill set for the job. So what do you say? And don't' worry, you'll enjoy a wonderful supper with me either way."

"Well, I have to admit that a challenge that gives my life meaning again would be most welcome," the captain said. "My house and my days are awfully empty since I lost Eleanor."

"Tuck, I need someone with your skills, experience, and temperament in that post," the president said. "So, I'm asking for your help in doing my best to steer this ship of state."

"Did you rehearse that line, Mr. President?" the captain asked with a grin.

"No, but it sounded pretty persuasive, didn't it?" the president asked with a grin of his own.

"Very persuasive," the captain agreed and extended his hand for a shake. "I accept … provided you'll allow me an extended learning curve."

"Learning curve?" the president echoed in a surprised tone. "From what I know and all that I've heard about you, it'll be your staff and I who will be learning."

"That's very kind of you, Mr. President," the captain said and shook the president's hand.

"Welcome aboard, Tuck!" the president boomed in his familiar way. "Let's eat!"

Well into the meal, the captain set his fork down, took a sip of ice water, and went to work.

"Mr. President," he said, "I'll be honest with you. Since Eleanor died, I felt my days were growing emptier by the day. But I already feel a new energy has been awakened by my accepting this new assignment. And I want you to know I'm honored and grateful that you trust me with it despite the difficulties I experienced at the end of my Navy career."

"I'm honored and grateful, too, Tuck," the president told him. "You had an exemplary and storied career over several decades. There's no way it could be diminished by a brief rough patch. You've emerged stronger and better than ever from what I'm sure was a dark time for you and Eleanor. But it's behind you—and now you've accepted this new opportunity to do the things you do best in further service to our nation. Believe me, it's a HUGE win-win!"

Feeling reconciled and rejuvenated, the captain's appetite came alive, and he dug into the prime rib, mashed sweet potatoes, and green beans while peppering the president with questions about the immediate and long-term military challenges ahead.

"So, Mr. President," the captain began, "what's the number one challenge I'll confront when I have a desk and phone?"

"Ironically, it's a new development I was briefed on only yesterday. We've discovered that China has at least twice as many nuclear-armed submarines as we thought. We've got very clear satellite images of a dozen 094A Jin Class subs clustered near the underwater entrance to an underground facility they swear does not exist on the western shore of Hainan Island, near their Yulin Naval Base.

"What's not at all clear is why China tipped its hand concerning six MIRV-carrying subs we didn't know they had and gave us proof their underground base not only exists but must be far larger and more sophisticated than we imagined.

"So our immediate challenge is to understand and quantify what we now know … and why the Chinese have allowed us to know it."

"It sounds like a vitally important challenge, alright," the captain agreed.

"But put it on the back burner while the related intelligence is still being gathered and analyzed," the president said. "Whatever more we may learn, the Chinese have given us a jarring look at the fearsome impact their military strategy is having … and an even more jarring look at how ours has fallen short. It's a recipe for defeat unless we can quickly upgrade and maximize training and technology, Tuck," the president explained. "Our military strategy must quickly become more forward-thinking, dynamic, and nimble. And I'm looking to you to help our commanders in every branch make that happen."

"Understood," the captain said emphatically. "I'd like to begin right away if I can, Mr. President. That is, if there's someone available at this hour with a grasp of strategy and tactics."

"I have just the man to help you get started!" the president said with a grin and led the captain down to the Situation Room, where Corporal Oliver was still hard at work, as the president had guessed he would be.

"Good evening, Corporal Oliver!" the president bellowed as he stepped from the elevator with his new senior advisor.

"Corporal Chance Oliver, meet my new Senior Advisor for Strategic Military Affairs, Captain Augustus Tucker Baird," the president said. "Corporal, I'd deeply appreciate your giving Captain Baird whatever time you have this evening to help him hit the ground running.

"And speaking of running, I still have several other priorities tonight. So I'll leave the two of you to break the ice and begin answering each other's questions. I'm excited to have you both collaborating on ideas that will help our military innovate a grand strategy for the future. I'm outta here now, but I'll send a car for you in the morning, Tuck, and we'll talk over breakfast. See you at 9:00 a.m.," the president said and disappeared into the elevator.

"Do you think he rehearsed that exit, Captain?" Chance asked.

"No, but it sure sounded like it, didn't it?" the captain replied. "And please call me Tuck," the captain said. "Formality retired when I did."

"Okay, Tuck," Chance said with a smile. "How much time do we have this evening?"

"However much time you have to give me," the captain replied.

"Well, I do have a commitment this evening," Chance said. "So, unfortunately, I only have a short while before I really must leave. Where would you like me to begin?"

"Well, for starters, who do you and your team support between situations?" the captain asked. "And how do you stay focused and on track with an ever-changing landscape?"

"Would you like to see what I call my 'Flash Card'?" Chance asked.

"For starters," the captain shot back.

"Intelligence in all its forms primarily comes to us from what we call the 'Big Five,'" Chance said as he clicked a remote to project his "Flash Card" onto a nearby wall.

Our Mission

Advise and serve the president by gathering, assessing, and sharing intel with

"The Big Five":

Central Intelligence Agency (CIA) trades in human intelligence to gather and analyze national security information from around the world.

National Reconnaissance Office (NRO), which designs, builds, launches, and operates U.S. reconnaissance satellites and disseminates satellite intelligence.

National Security Agency (NSA), which conducts worldwide mass data collection and bugs foreign electronic communications.

Defense Intelligence Agency (DIA), which collects and analyzes military-related foreign political, economic, industrial, geographic, and medical intelligence.

National Geospatial-Intelligence Agency (NGA), which creates collects, analyzes, and distributes maps and other geospatial intelligence.

Our Strategy

1. *Coordinate, analyze, report, and secure intelligence we receive from, and exchange with, "The Big Five" and the military*
2. *Devise faster, more efficient, more secure methods to accomplish #1.*

"That's an amazing distillation of complex roles and concepts into easy-to-understand info," the captain marveled. "But how do you organize what you exchange with them?"

"We provide military brass what I call 'T.A.C.K.S.,'" Chance said and tapped his remote.

Brass T.A.C.K.S.

T heories

A ssumptions

C onclusions

K nowledge

S uspicions

"We collect, analyze, catalog, and share theories, assumptions, and conclusions used by the Big Five and the military to maximize usable knowledge ... which forms a basis for suspicions and effective counter-strategies."

"I'm very impressed!" the captain said sincerely. "But I don't see 'Facts' anywhere."

"Neither do we," Chance chuckled. "Under close inspection, we often find that so-called 'facts' are little more than someone's theories, assumptions, or conclusions in disguise. So we organize them under 'Knowledge.'"

"Point taken!" the captain replied. "Corporal Oliver, I believe we have a starting point!"

"Then let's call it a day—or more accurately, a night—and pick it up from here in the morning, after your breakfast with the president," Chance proposed.

"It's a deal!" the captain agreed and shook Chance's hand.

"You may want to wear dress blues again tomorrow for your ID badge," Chance suggested. "Aside from that, we're pretty casual around here—as you've no doubt noticed."

"So noted," the captain replied, then shook Chance's hand and headed to the elevator.

7

THE PRODIGAL DAUGHTER

President Prescott's new Senior Advisor for Strategic Military Affairs slept soundly that first night of his appointment. It was his first good night's sleep since his wife died nearly four months earlier. For the first time in weeks, he spent most of it in bed, after dozing for two hours in his favorite easy chair with Margo, his wife's rescued tabby, asleep in his lap.

The captain awoke in the chair when Margo jumped to the floor shortly after 11:00 that peaceful night, and he was pleased to feel as though he could sleep for a few more hours. So he hung his robe on its hook in his wardrobe and quickly fell back asleep beneath the covers in the old four-poster bed his Eleanor had purchased during one of her many expeditions to antique shops and thrift stores in and around Alexandria.

By 7:00 the next morning, he gave his Navy dress blue uniform a quick once-over in the full-length, beveled mirror Eleanor had him fasten to the inside of the door of their walk-in closet. He smiled when he recalled her response when he told her they could afford a new mirror and that she didn't need to settle for this old one she'd found in her favorite thrift store.

"I don't settle for anything in life, my love!" she said with her bewitching smile. "I didn't settle for less than the very best when I selected the man I would marry. So why on Earth would I settle when it comes to picking a mirror?"

The captain gently ran a hand along the top of the mirror and thought about how grateful he was that Eleanor loved the way she did ... and how grateful he was to have been loved by her. As he slowly closed the closet door, the doorbell rang, and the captain checked his watch.

The car's here early, he thought and hustled downstairs to answer the door.

"I should have known you'd be early!" he said as he opened the dark oak front door.

"Hi, Uncle Tuck!" the captain's wayward niece said with a smile as dazzling as when he'd last seen her, nearly ten years earlier. "Oh my, you do look handsome in that uniform."

"Aubrey Lynn?!" he said softly. "Is it really you?! Oh, my word, my prayers have been answered!" the captain exclaimed as his niece hurried into his open arms.

"What do you mean you should have known I'd be

early?" she asked. "How did you even know I was coming? I was so looking forward to surprising you."

"Oh, I'm awaiting a driver to take me to a breakfast appointment this morning," the captain explained. "But I don't expect the car for another half-hour. So when I heard the doorbell, I just assumed it was my driver. When what to my wondering eyes should appear, but my beloved niece from whom I feared I might never again hear!"

"That's awfully stilted poetry, Uncle Tuck," Aubrey giggled, "and it's also a shameless act of plagiarism if you ask me."

"It will never stand up in court," the captain chuckled. "The world can't even agree if that line was written by Clement Clarke Moore or Henry Livingston Jr. So I'm safe. Have you had breakfast yet?"

"Actually, I had hoped to be able to take you and Aunt Eleanor to breakfast and begin to catch up on our lives," Aubrey said with a hint of disappointment. "But I'm willing to change that to lunch sometime after your appointment."

"Well, we certainly do have much to catch up on," the captain sighed. "But how about if we begin by bringing you along to my breakfast meeting and then spending the day together? I'd really like that. We have do have an awful lot to catch up on."

"Oh, I don't want to impose on your meeting," Aubrey told her uncle.

"Nonsense!" the captain insisted with a huge grin. "I think you'd really enjoy coming along. After all, it's not every day that you get to have breakfast at the White House."

"The White House?" Aubrey blurted out. "You're having breakfast with the president?"

"Just this once," the captain said with a grin. "So I wouldn't miss it if I were you."

"Well ... well ... of course I'll go if you're sure it will be alright," Aubrey said.

"I'm certain of it," the captain told her. "The president was a friend of your father's, and I just know he will appreciate meeting you."

"But I don't have anything to wear, and my hair's a mess," Aubrey said more to herself than to her uncle.

"Aubrey, he's not that kind of president," the captain assured her. "He'll welcome you with open arms, believe me."

"Then I'll go." She smiled brightly again. "But I have to freshen up before we leave."

The captain grabbed her two suitcases from the porch and led her to the first-floor guest bedroom. He smiled as he watched her rummage through her cosmetics case for a hairbrush and just the right makeup. The sight brought a tear to his eye as he recalled watching Eleanor do the very same things many times.

"It's a wonderful surprise to have you here, Aubrey," the captain told her quietly, as he leaned against the door-frame of the guest room. "It's been such a long time since you visited."

"I know I should have let you know I was coming, but this was a sudden decision, and I wanted to surprise the two of you," Aubrey said. "Is Aunt Eleanor going with us?"

"I'm afraid not," the captain said and suddenly saddened. "She was so very proud of you, Aubrey. She searched for any news she could find of you online, and she rejoiced when you earned your Ph.D. at MIT."

"What do you mean she was proud of me?" Aubrey asked with a pained expression. "I know my rebellious-ness must have disappointed her along with you and Father. But I never meant to hurt anyone. I just had to break free of the cocoon Father had me wrapped so tightly within. I had to break free and find out who I really am. I know that doesn't excuse my awful anger and silence when the two of you reached out and tried so hard to stay in touch. I feel terrible about being so thoughtless and immature about that for so long. I just hope she understands that I was young and overly emotional. And I hope to make it up to you both now that I'm back home."

"You mean you're back to stay?" the captain asked excitedly. "Forever?"

"Well, none of us is here forever," Aubrey said, almost flippantly.

The captain's mood instantly grew darker, and he went silent.

"Did I say something wrong, Uncle Tuck?" Aubrey asked urgently. "Are you alright?"

"I'm very sad to tell you that you've returned just a few months too late, my dear," the captain said as he held her by the shoulders.

In the next heartbeat, Aubrey put it all together: the quietness of the house, the captain's mixed emotions about her surprise reappearance—and the obvious impact of her statement about no one being here forever.

"Oh, Uncle Tuck! No! Not Aunt Eleanor! Not now!" Aubrey almost screamed. "Not when I've finally grown up and come back to thank her for all she did for me after Mother died when I was so very young! I can't accept it! I can't! I can't!"

The captain held his niece tightly in his arms and ran his hand over her long auburn hair as he had so many times when she was a young girl and had another argument of many arguments with her father. It quickly soothed her then—but it didn't that morning in the house Aubrey never dreamed would one day lose the light that shined from her Aunt Eleanor's heart.

"Oh, Uncle Tuck! I'm so, so sorry for not being here to thank her, to tell her goodbye, to be here for her ... and for you." Aubrey could hardly speak as she struggled to catch her breath.

"It's okay, dear heart," the captain told her softly and continued to hold her and run his hand over her hair. "Your Aunt Eleanor is at peace, and we're here for each other. And now that we are, we must continue to be. That's what matters. Your light brightened this house the instant I opened the front door and saw you standing there."

The familiar gleaming black Suburban pulled up in front of the captain's house at precisely 8:30, and a Marine corporal took the eight front steps two at a time, straightened his cap using his reflection in the full-length glass of the storm door, and rang the bell.

"Good morning! Looking sharp, sir!" the corporal said cheerfully after he and the captain exchanged quick, crisp salutes.

"Good morning, Corporal," the captain replied as he led his niece out the door. "This is my niece, the highly intelligent and exceedingly beautiful Ms. Aubrey Lynn Baird. Please advise the White House that I'm bringing her along as my guest this morning."

"Yes, sir!" the corporal replied approvingly as he gazed

at Aubrey briefly before he hustled back to the Suburban and held the rear door open while she and her uncle climbed in. "Captain Baird is bringing his niece, Ms. Aubrey Baird, as an added breakfast guest this morning. Our ETA is 8:50," he said into his phone before the SUV reached the end of the captain's block.

"Well, Uncle," Aubrey said with a twinkle in her eye, "you have certainly out-surprised me this morning. I'm now actually thrilled that I haven't eaten yet. Have you eaten at the White House before? Is it a normal break-fast, a continental breakfast, or just coffee, juice, and some kind of pastry? Do you know if Melania is joining us?"

The captain had to laugh at the barrage of questions his niece sent flying his way. He was pleased that the surprise of breakfast with the president seemed to have at least temporarily overshadowed his niece's shock and grief of learning that his wife, her only aunt, had died. The pair reached Camilla's desk minutes before 9:00, just enough time for her to walk them to the Map Room.

"You must be Aubrey!" Camilla said with a broad smile. "It's so nice to meet you. Your father was so proud of you. He bragged about you every time he was here," she said.

"Thank you very much," Aubrey replied. "I'm thrilled to meet you, um …."

"Just call me Camilla, dear," the president's secretary

told her. "We're pretty informal around here among good friends."

"Well, I'm very pleased to meet you, Camilla," Aubrey said.

"Good morning to you also, Captain Baird," Camilla said with a lilt. "Please follow me, and I'll get the two of you seated before the president comes rushing out of his Daily Briefing."

"Good morning, Camilla," the captain replied, and he and his niece followed her to the Map Room, where a small, round dining table was set and waiting for them.

The captain had just enough time to take his first sip of ice water when President Prescott walked through the door with his trademark smile on full display

"This job comes with many surprises, but few are as pleasant as finally having the pleasure of meeting the accomplished and attractive young woman I've heard so very much about," the president boomed. "Good morning and welcome to the White House, Ms. Aubrey Lynn Baird," the president boomed happily and briefly held Aubrey by her shoulders. "Your father always talked glowingly about you. He was very proud of you, and I can understand why."

"It's an honor to meet you, President Prescott," Aubrey replied. "You're doing a wonderful job for the American people and for American businesses. You must be proud as well."

"I'm just doing what I came to Washington to do," the president said simply. "And thanks to the talented and able people, like your uncle, around me, we're getting more done every day. But hey, I'm starving. Daily Briefings always make me hungry. Let's eat!"

The buffet of scrambled eggs, baked parmesan hash brown potatoes, thick-sliced smoked bacon, ham, hickory-smoked sausage links, mini hotcakes, sliced tomatoes, fruit, and melon was over the top, and Aubrey marveled at the sight of the president eating a little of everything.

She smiled subtly at the sight of him enthusiastically eating with a linen napkin tucked neatly into the collar of his lavender Ledbury shirt to protect his "D.J. Prescott" designer silk necktie and his Brooks Brothers Golden Fleece suit (Navy blue in honor of the captain, no doubt).

Not long into the meal, the president suddenly put down his fork and knife, took a sip of ice water, glanced at the captain for a moment, then thoughtfully fixed his gaze on Aubrey.

"My dear," he began, then paused another moment. "I hope I didn't offend or upset you when I spoke of your father a few minutes ago. I want you to know that whatever you may have heard about his last days, he was a close and valued friend through thick and thin for many years … and nothing could ever diminish that in my heart and mind.

"I hope you'll forgive me for failing to express my condolences when I greeted you," he continued. "Frankly, I'm still getting used to the news of his passing."

"It's okay, Mr. President, really," Aubrey said with a poise that surprised the captain. "Thank you for so many kind words about him. You're not the first, by any means, to tell me how good and true a friend he was. To be honest, I'm the one who probably should apologize for the stories you've no doubt heard concerning my immaturity and ingratitude during my teens and twenties.

"But I've returned home a bit wiser, and I plan to honor my father's business and philanthropic legacy to the best of my abilities," Aubrey said with determination in her voice. "And you so graciously hosting me here this morning, thanks to the friendship you enjoyed with my father, has put a fine point on the size of the challenge ahead."

"It sounds like you plan to assume the helm of your father's various enterprises," the president said. "That will be a monumental undertaking, I'm sure. But you are definitely your father's daughter. So I'm equally sure that you are up to the task."

"Does this mean you're home to stay?" the captain excitedly asked.

"It does!" Aubrey replied. "And you and I have much to discuss in the days ahead!"

"Now I'm really hungry!" the captain said and attacked his eggs. "Mr. President, I'm afraid I won't be in today. I know it's not an advisable approach to one's first day on the job. But I'm sure you understand how extenuating my extenuating circumstances are this morning."

"I understand completely," the president assured him. "But I really must insist that you at least stick around long enough for pictures. I've asked Camilla to have the White House photographer set up in the next room so that we can quickly get your staff ID photo out of the way, then pose for a few together. I'd greatly appreciate that, if you don't mind, Ms. Baird."

"Mind?!" Aubrey exclaimed. "I've been sitting here trying to gather the nerve to ask you to pose for a selfie with us! What a treat this is! And *please*, Mr. President, call me Aubrey."

"Sounds like a fair exchange," the president said.

"So, what is this new job, Uncle Tuck?" Aubrey asked with interest.

"Your uncle has thankfully agreed to serve as my Senior Advisor for Strategic Military Affairs," the president cut in.

"Wow! Really? How interesting … and exciting, I'm sure," Aubrey replied. "I'm honored to get top priority today, for sure."

"Every day, my dear," the captain said softly and placed a hand on hers. "Every day."

"Well, are we ready for pictures?" the president looked at his watch and said.

"Give me a moment to freshen up, please, and I'll be right back," Aubrey said.

"She's quite a tribute to her father," the president told the captain when she left.

"That she is, Mr. President," the captain agreed. "And I believe we don't yet know the half of it."

"So what would you like to do today?" the captain asked during the ride back to Alexandria.

"I'm not sure," Aubrey replied. "I think for starters, I'd like to take Aunt Eleanor some flowers. I know she loved white roses. And I'd love to plant some at her graveside if the cemetery allows it."

"They do," the captain told her. "And I'd planned to do just that this weekend. Let's do it together today instead. I'd like that. I believe your Aunt Eleanor will like it very much too."

When they returned to the captain's house in Alexandria's historic Old Town district, he donned jeans and a flannel shirt before he and Aubrey jumped into his Lincoln Aviator and headed to the Soft Petal Nursery. Aubrey picked out a pair of hearty white rose bushes, potting soil, plant food, gardening tools, and a watering can, and they headed to St. Paul's Cemetery.

St. Paul's was not very big, and the captain parked the Lincoln just steps from Eleanor's grave and just a few more steps away from the Grave of the Female Stranger. It was the first thing Aubrey saw as Lincoln rolled to a stop.

"Oh my!" she said softly. "Is that what I think it is?" she asked her uncle.

"It is if you're thinking it's the Grave of the Female Stranger," he told her.

"And here's Aunt Eleanor's grave! How did you manage to arrange this?" Aubrey asked.

"I have a friend of a friend of a friend of someone who manages the cemetery," the captain explained. "I knew your aunt would love being this close to the Female Stranger if it were possible. So when I learned that a friend of mine was owed a favor, well, I guess you could say I bought his I.O.U."

"Well, I know it's where she would want to be at rest if there were any way possible," Aubrey told her uncle. "So I'm very pleased that you found a way. And I believe she is too."

"After hearing your aunt talk about the Female Stranger for years and learning the 'Lady's' story, I knew there was only one place for the two of us to ultimately come to rest. It gives me a certain peace."

"Unless Father had specific wishes for such an eventuality, I think I'd like to bring him here when we find him,"

Aubrey told her uncle. "What do you think, Uncle Tuck?"

"I never heard him speak about it, that's for sure, so unless he made his wishes known in his will, I'd say this is a good place to bring him. I know I'd like him close to me—when that day comes, that is."

"Yes, when that day comes," Aubrey repeated. "Do you think there's a chance he's still alive, Uncle Tuck?"

"Until we know otherwise, I do believe there's a chance, dear one," the captain told her.

"Me too," Aubrey said and hugged her uncle's arm tight.

"What do you say we make your Aunt Eleanor happy with these new rose bushes and then go spend the day together in her honor?" the captain proposed.

"Sounds perfect!" Aubrey said, and the two of them went to work planting the roses.

8

A BLESSING IN DISGUISE

The captain rose early the next morning, eager to begin his first day on the job. He brewed a pot of dark roast coffee, put two blueberry scones in the toaster oven, then quickly showered, shaved, and dressed in jeans and a black turtleneck sweater. The welcome aroma of coffee roused Aubrey from her sleep in the guest room near the kitchen, and she slipped into a robe and slippers to join her uncle in the hope of enjoying a cup with him before he left.

"Good morning!" she said softly as she shuffled into the kitchen, headed directly for the pot of coffee on the stove.

"Good morning, Dear One!" her uncle said, happy to have a few minutes with her before the SUV arrived to whisk him to work. "Did you sleep well?"

"Better than I think I've slept in years," she answered and found a cup where she remembered they were kept.

"I'm not surprised," the captain said. "That's been your bed since your first sleepover with us when you were four years old, and it was always tough to get you up in the morning."

"It was marvelous to awaken to the smell of fresh-brewed coffee," she said as she poured herself a large cup.

"I warmed an extra blueberry scone in case you got up and joined me," the captain said as he pulled on a pair of black cherry Cody James western boots. "It's in the toaster oven."

"You're an angel," Aubrey said and took a long sip of coffee before retrieving the scone.

The captain's cell phone vibrated atop the counter, and a photo of the Suburban lit up the screen, which the captain tapped to acknowledge he got the message.

"Well, it's time for me to go and help save the world for all humanity," he chuckled. "That's the only thing that can tear me from spending another entire day with you, Aubrey."

"I guess I'll manage somehow." She feigned a sigh and took a bite of her scone. "One thing I'll probably do is stop by the bakery where you bought this. Where'd you get it?"

"It's a terrific little bakery just blocks from here on Mount Vernon Avenue, called 'We Knead the Dough!'" her uncle told her. "You may want to pick up a couple of loaves of bread too. My keys are on the hook next to the side door. The Lincoln's got nearly a full tank of gas, and my bike's right beside it in the garage. I promise to get off as early as possible today. After all, how intense can my first day be, right?"

"Better knock on wood when you make a statement like that," Aubrey chuckled and poured another cup of coffee. "Can I pick up anything else for you while I'm out today?"

"Nope, just think about where you'd like to go to supper when I get back," he told her.

"I think I'll leave that up to you," she replied. "Call me when you're on the way home."

"I'll do that," the captain replied and paused another moment to say, "It's great having you here, Dear One. See you soon!"

"See you soon," she echoed and hugged him goodbye before he headed out to the SUV waiting for him in the driveway.

Still sleepy despite the coffee, Aubrey decided to curl up in a living room recliner with a cozy throw her Aunt Eleanor had finished knitting the day before she died. She was asleep in minutes and dreamed of her father.

That first official morning, the Marine who opened the Suburban's door for the captain under the West Wing portico walked him to his new office, just steps from the Oval. He sat in his new leather chair just long enough to find the Situation Room's extension and called to let Corporal Oliver know he was headed down to meet with him. As the captain had hoped, his retinal scan and palm print were already in the system, so he used the elevator without a hitch.

"Good morning, Corporal!" the captain said to Chance cheerfully. "I've finally made it!"

"That you have, sir," Chance said with a smile and a salute with shoulders back.

"Let's dispense with saluting, Corporal," the captain proposed. "It's going to be difficult enough for me to blend in around here as it is. So you be 'Chance,' and I'll be 'Tuck.' Deal?"

"Deal!" Chance agreed with a relieved look on his young face.

"So, where would you like to begin in understanding what goes on here?" Chance asked.

"Actually, Chance, I'm hoping to take a broader view, which I believe you can help me gain and keep in focus," the captain replied.

"I'll do my best, sir … er, I mean Tuck," Chance corrected himself awkwardly.

"In the simplest possible terms, I see the Situation Room as the critical crossroads for the intel earmarked for the president by the Big Five you spoke of the evening before last," Tuck stated.

"That's a fair characterization," Chance agreed. "But our team does far more than simply pass information along. The president looks to us for the support he needs to address situations. Whether we receive the information as human or technological intel, whether the format is hard copy or digital, recorded or live, President Prescott comes to us needing and expecting the clearest possible looks at situations he's confronting,

"The president doesn't come to us looking for advice," Chance explained. "He depends upon us to have the latest information and the best possible understanding of what additional information he needs … and where and how to get it."

"Oh, is that all?" the captain asked with reverence.

"Oh, there's one more thing," Chance said soberly. "Actually, at the worst of times, there's two more things: Time is running out … and lives are at stake."

"That said, let's take a step back in the process," Tuck suggested. "Give me an idea of where the information comes from. Like, for instance, our recent look at those Chinese subs."

"Well, those images came from the NRO, the National Reconnaissance Office," Chance said. "They design, build, launch, and operate all U.S. reconnaissance satellites."

"All of them?" Tuck asked to be clear.

"All of them," Chance confirmed.

"How do they accomplish that?" Tuck pressed.

"I'll try to keep it simple," Chance warned the captain. "NRO Director Alexander Riddle coordinates collection and analysis of information from airplane and satellite reconnaissance by the military services and the CIA. The agency is supported by about 3,000 federal personnel, comprised of an NRO cadre and others within the National Geospatial-Intelligence Agency and the National Security Agency, plus the Air Force, Army, Navy, and CIA."

"That's a lot of people," Tuck said.

"It's the tip of the freaking iceberg, Tuck," Chance advised him. "According to the General Accounting Office, the NRO has the largest budget of the Big Five that we talked about the other day. Most of the financials are classified. But the portion that's not pays for 'tens of thousands' of defense contractor personnel, who perform all the analysis."

"You walk around with all that in your head?" Tuck asked with some amazement.

"Well, it's a bit deeper than that, but you've got the CliffsNotes version," Chance said with a slight grin. "And there's an equal portion for each of the others in the Big Five. Keeping it straight and up to date gives me a headache sometimes ... but I like to know who we're dancing with when the music starts down here. You know what I mean?"

"I think I do," Tuck answered sincerely. "So when you receive intel from NRO or one of the other agencies, do you ever wonder about the quality of the baseline data and/or analysis?"

"Of course," Chance sighed. "I always try to keep it front-of-mind because in the end, no matter how many hundreds of billions of dollars are invested in people, technology, and logistics, no matter how many ground-breaking advances are made, we're cursed with the same damned limitation as every fourth-grader with a laptop."

"What's that?" Tuck asked.

"Garbage in, garbage out!" Chance answered with a shrug.

"At 299,792,458 meters per second. That's quite a thought, isn't it?" Tuck said with a feeble grin. "Do you have any way of knowing what's garbage before you put it in?"

"President Ronald Reagan used to like to say, 'Trust, but verify.'" Chance said with a weary grin. "We wish we had that luxury. We have to trust our sources. I mean, let's face it; even if we had the means to verify the quality of the intel we get, we almost never have the time it would require before the president needs to review it. So the truth is we often have a greater feeling of control when we buy produce than when we receive intel that will influence the decisions of the most powerful man in the free world. That's your daily dose of reality, Tuck," Chance said to wrap up the subject.

"It's a little unsettling," Tuck replied.

"Don't let it do that to you, Tuck," Chance advised with a hand on the captain's shoulder. "Keep it in perspective. Are you married?"

"I was," Tuck answered. "For nearly forty years, before the Good Lord took her home."

"Well then, you'll know what I'm talking about when I say working here is a lot like being married," Chance philosophized, "When all is said and done, it comes down to trust. Except down here, circumstances often change at the rate of 299,792,458 meters per second."

"Why 299,792,458 meters per second?" Tuck asked.

"That's the speed of light," Chance explained.

"If my Eleanor were here, she'd tell you that can happen in a marriage too," Tuck said with thoughts of the *USS Ronald Reagan* incident. *It's funny, and a little Shakespearean, the way Ronald Reagan came up twice while we talked about trust,* he thought.

"So while we're talking about the quality of the intel you receive, can I see the latest images you have of the Chinese subs?" Tuck asked.

"Sure!" Chance said and quickly called the images up using his keyboard.

Tuck leaned in close for a good look at Chance's monitor.

"Can you put them up on the big screen?" Tuck asked.

"You got it," Chance shot back, and the images were projected on a floor-to-ceiling screen behind Tuck in the blink of an eye.

"Whoa!" Tuck exclaimed. "Those are clear images, alright!"

"The clearest we've ever seen down here," Chance told him.

"They're amazing!" Tuck said in awe as he strode up to the wall for a closer look as Chance clicked through the 18 images.

"Agreed!" Chance said. "They're almost too good to be true."

"What do you mean by that?" Tuck pressed him.

"Well, they're easily the clearest, most-detailed we've ever received," Chance explained.

"Can you account for that?" Tuck asked.

"What do you mean?" Chance asked in response.

"Do you understand why they're so much clearer?" Tuck pressed for more info.

"Not really," Chance replied. "But it's obviously a good thing."

"I suppose," Tuck said. "But I think it would be an equally good thing if we were to be routinely briefed on technological advancements that improve intel quality and delivery."

"If I may, Tuck, the key word there is 'routinely,'" Chance explained. "We are currently briefed twice a year on the newest—and upcoming—improvements."

"But in the meantime, you have no idea whether the next satellite images you receive will or not be of equal quality—or better."

"With all due respect, Tuck, we could never be sure of that regardless of how often we're briefed," Chance reasoned. "The quality of the intel we receive, particularly satellite imagery, is dependent on more than the technology used to capture and transmit it. There's no accounting for atmospheric conditions, system problems, even solar wind. What we do know is that we get the best intel available at the moment."

"I don't take issue with any of that, Chance," Tuck replied. "I'm merely suggesting that your team—and the president—might be even better-served as improvements to methods and means occur, rather than as late as six months afterward. It's essentially the same strategy that I personally experienced a month ago, during the tragic events involving my brother. I marveled at the way your team seamlessly melded and maximized the technology at your fingertips with human intelligence on the ground."

"That was a real-world example of the best work we do here when the information we need is available," Chance explained.

"That's my point exactly, Chance," Tuck pressed the matter. "And given your confidence in the amount and accuracy of the available information, I'm certain your team is confident it can duplicate the outcome, should the need arise again. My point is that your team should be tuned in to the cutting edge of what each of the Big Five is capable of delivering before you need it.

"It's not a perfect example, but a similar scenario unfolded in the spring of 1960 when the Soviet Union shot down Francis Gary Powers' U-2 spy plane," Tuck explained. "The C-75 surface-to-air missile the Soviets used was that era's shot heard around the world. It proved we were spying on the Soviets from the air, and it cost Powers two years in a Soviet prison camp."

"I know where you're going with this," Chance cut in. "While some segments of the U.S. military held their breath, thinking the U.S. had not only lost a U-2 and a prized pilot—but had also lost its ability to know what the Soviet military was up to—our intelligence community didn't lose sleep because we were about to launch our first-generation Corona spy satellite."

"So you get where I'm coming from," the captain happily summarized.

"To a degree," Chance conceded. "But that occurred more than half a century ago. Our advances in means and methods occur far faster today."

"And now it seems they progress at 299,792,458 meters per second, right?" Tuck quipped.

"Exactly!" Chance said with a sigh.

"And that's exactly the basis I'll use for my case when I propose to the president that we change our briefing strategy," Tuck told him.

Chance was about to say something but stopped short because his watch began vibrating.

"I probably don't have to tell you this," he said to Tuck, "but your timing is flawless."

"Why do you say that?" Tuck asked innocently.

"The president's on his way down," Chance said and led the way to the elevator.

"Good morning, Mr. President," Chance said and saluted as the president entered the room.

"Good morning, sir," Tuck said.

"Good morning, gentlemen," the president said with a serious look on his face and led the pair in the direction of a soundproof side room. "Follow me, please."

"What's up, Mr. President?" Chance asked as the president closed the door behind them.

"I learned something very disturbing in today's Daily Briefing," the president replied. "I asked for an update on the Chinese nuclear subs we recently learned about, and I was told we've lost six of the twelve. Not surprisingly, we can't find the six that were secretly built right under our noses. What is surprising … no, I mean what's goddamned shocking, is that I had to ask! We can't see them with our satellites! We can't hear them with our hydrophones! It's like they just vanished! Like they don't even exist! But does anyone tell the president? Sure … if he asks!"

"If they've eluded our hydrophones, China has a whole new fish in the sea," Tuck said and looked at Chance for input.

"I'm afraid you're right, Tuck," Chance agreed. "We've never had problems tracking the first six because they make so much noise. Which begs the question of why the first six haven't been retrofitted with the quieter engineering the new six appear to have.

"But back to the question of where they're at: We know where they were 48 hours ago," Chance thought out loud. "And we know they have a maximum cruising speed of 20 knots."

"Let's not duplicate effort," the president said. "NRO's already hunting for them. Besides, I have a suspicion all six are once again moored in that secret base under Hainan Island. Which begs a couple of tough questions: Why don't we know for sure? And what are our multi-billion-dollar spy satellites actually worth?"

"Don't be too hard on our eyes in the sky, Mr. President," Tuck said in an effort to turn the discussion in the direction of strategy. "Those images we have are photographs, not video captures. It's easy to imagine the subs were on the surface just long enough for one of our LEOs to catch sight of them, and its onboard computer opted to snap still shots instead of video. I will concede that it's odd we didn't capture any shots of the subs submerging. But once they did, it would have been a simple matter for them to quickly slip back into the underground base."

"Chance, standby for an update from NRO … and call me immediately when you get it."

"Will do, Mr. President," Chance replied confidently. "We'll locate them, sir."

"Tuck, I need to run a couple of things by you one-on-one," the president said when Chance exited the room. "Give my your take on why President Liú might travel halfway around the world to proclaim he has no plans of nuclear aggression only to race back to China and reveal a nuclear force neither we nor any other nation in the world ever imagined he had? If you were trying to convince me that you mean me no harm, would you do it while waving a loaded gun in my face—a gun I never knew you had?"

"Maybe that's not what President Liú did?" Tuck suggested.

"What the hell is that supposed to mean?" the president asked in exasperation.

"Do you know what all your military commanders are doing at all times?" Tuck asked.

"How on Earth could I?" the president shot back, even more exasperated by the thought.

"How could anyone?" Tuck posited. "Even President Liú?"

"So you're guessing, Liú's facing some sort of military power grab? A potential coup?" the president pressed his newest advisor.

"Now is not the time to guess," Tuck said flatly. "But neither is it the time to assume."

"So what do you propose I do?" the President asked, intrigued by Tuck's counsel.

"Give President Liú an innocent follow-up call," Tuck suggested. "Thank him again for his visit and his assurances regarding peace. Just one friend to another. Don't reveal what we know about the subs. But slip in an offhand remark about how assurances like the one he gave you boost your efforts to convince our military leadership that we're on the right course to a lasting peace. Perhaps it will elicit a comment from him—a hint of hostile military pressures he's dealing with. Who knows, he may open up a little if you catch him at the right moment. If he does, we'll have a greater insight into China's internal affairs—in which case, this O94A incident could actually prove to be a blessing in disguise."

"Not a bad idea, Tuck," the president said with his first smile of the morning. "Remind me to give you a raise."

"I'll do that, Mr. President," Tuck chuckled, "at some strategically opportune time. You said you had two things to run by me. What's the other one?"

"You should probably have a seat for this one," the president advised.

"You mean you've saved the worst for last?" Tuck replied, trying to keep things light.

"Well, it's the best as far as you and Aubrey are concerned," the president answered. "Jonah's alive."

"WHAT?" Tuck exclaimed so loud, he was glad they were in a soundproof room. "Why the hell didn't you tell me this first?"

"Purely selfish reasons, I will admit," the president answered. "I needed you to have a clear head to address the China question. How clear is your head at the moment?"

"Point made," Tuck shot back.

The president slid a manila envelope across the table to Tuck. The captain opened the envelope and pulled out a fuzzy 8"x 10" black and white photo of his brother.

"That photo was taken of him early this morning at an ATM in lower Manhattan," the president said. "The FBI put it through their facial recognition system. He's pretty haggard and could use a shave, but we're sure it's Jonah. But frankly, we know little more than that.

"Yesterday, your brother was discovered hiding aboard a boat being stored at a marina at the south end of Gravesend Bay. There are usually fifty or more boats in storage there, and the one Jonah picked to hide in just happens to belong to Colonel Matthew Winters, Commander of the Fort Hamilton Army Garrison, at the north end of the bay. Your brother had apparently been laying low there, panhandling since his copter crashed in the Hudson.

"Rather than call the cops like a normal citizen, the soft-hearted colonel decided to play Good Samaritan and took your brother back to the Garrison, let him shower, gave him a change of clothes, a hot meal, and a warm, comfortable bed for the night. He figured he'd call someone in the morning and hook Jonah up with a local shelter. But early this morning, your brother was gone. Security at the Garrison isn't the greatest when it comes to keeping people in.

"Anyway, about a half-hour later, your brother hitched a ride with a kindhearted commuter on the Belt Parkway, who took him into lower Manhattan. Jonah then strong-armed the motorist and made off with the guy's ATM card and PIN. A camera at the ATM snapped that photo of him while he withdrew the $500 maximum.

"New York PD shared the photo with the FBI," the president told him. "The Bureau ran it through their facial recognition software and got a hit on Jonah. They've issued an all-points bulletin on him and called Jasper to alert us that they believe they're closing in on him. Two NYPD detectives were at the FBI field office in the Javitz Federal Building this morning, running downloads from every street camera within five miles of the ATM through their FR software. If he's on the streets, we'll catch him."

"What if he's hooked up with some of his henchmen?" Tuck asked plaintively. "What then?"

"God only knows," the president said softly. "I've got some of my best people working on it. And when we finish this conversation, I'm going straight up to the Oval to call Doc. I expect to have him on the case by this afternoon. If Jonah's alive, Doc will find him. In the meantime, you are going home to gently break the news to Aubrey. She's going to need you near. So I'm not expecting you back here today. Understood?"

"Understood," Tuck sighed. "Thank you, Mr. President," Tuck said sincerely. "Wish me luck and pray I find the words."

"I have no doubt you will," the president assured him. "And thank you for your counsel on the China matter, Tuck."

9

BACK FROM THE DEAD

People fishing on Flathead Lake that morning got quite a show as Doc and Q raced their twin two-seater Icon A5 seaplanes around the lake about 500 feet in the air. The sleek, white planes gleamed in the morning sun and toyed with one another like young, carefree sea birds. Thomas Byrnes rode along with Doc. His brother Raymon sat beside Q. It was their first experience in small planes—not to mention planes that soared to 3,000 feet at 250 miles per hour, then swooped low, just above the tops of the pines that ring the lake and finally approached the surface of the lake, slowed to 100 miles per hour, then silently came to rest on the clear, placid water.

"Wow! What a ride!" Raymon shouted excitedly as Q threw open the canopy to enjoy the cool morning air. "Do you fellas do this every day?" Raymon asked him.

"I wish," Q sighed. "Most mornings, Doc goes out rowing by his self at sunrise. I've always been a night owl, so I'm usually just falling asleep about the time he starts out."

"This flight was special just for you and this stick-in-the-mud brother of yours," Doc said as he guided his Icon in close to Q's and lashed them loosely together. "I've got some worms and tackle behind my seat in case you two would like to fish a little."

"What fish are in here?" Thomas made the mistake of asking.

Q was thrilled that he asked.

"Northern Pike, Mountain Whitefish, Kokanee Salmon, Yellow Perch, Largemouth Bass, Smallmouth Bass, and Sturgeon," he recited just as he had memorized them.

"No trout?" Thomas made the additional mistake of asking, and Doc shook his head.

"A few," Q said with a grin, then rattled off "Brown Trout, Lake Trout, Golden Trout, Brook Trout, Bull Trout, Rainbow Trout … and Cutthroat Trout."

"I love trout," Thomas said eagerly.

"You don't have a fishing license," Raymon reminded him.

"Just keep your eyes peeled for the game warden," Q said with a chuckle. "If you see him coming, we'll pack up and take off. It drives him crazy every time."

When the brothers both had a couple of lines in the

water, Q sat beside Doc and asked, "What were you lookin' for when you followed the road on our second loop around the lake?"

"Nothing," Doc answered him simply.

"There's nothing to see over the road unless you're looking for somebody on it." Q pressed his friend for the answer he already knew. "You were looking for strangers, weren't you? Maybe Guardians? Did you see any? I didn't. I think they're on their last legs without Jonah Baird to tell 'em what to do next … and pay for it. So I doubt they're much interested in harassing us anymore."

"I hope you're right, Q," Doc replied quietly. "I don't want to stir that pot while the brothers are still here. The last thing they need is another wild goose chase. After catching Mancini's crew at St. John's, I believe he's not sure where Baird has hidden his loot. And I know he can't possibly be as big a threat without it. But I'm not convinced he'll give up easily. And you can bet he's pissed at us for snatching that gold and silver from the bunch he sent to find it. And who's to say he doesn't have money from some other Baird stash?"

"We've got company!" Raymon said as he and Thomas pulled their lines out of the lake.

Doc's head swiveled, and he saw four speedboats coming toward them at full speed from four directions.

"There's never been four wardens on this lake, Doc," Q

said warily. "Hell, I don't believe there are four of 'em in this region."

As the boats closed in, Doc could see they weren't with Montana Fish, Wildlife & Parks.

"T-minus ten seconds and counting!" he announced, then hurriedly untethered the planes and helped the brothers toss the fishing tackle behind his seat. "I'll straighten the lines out later!" he shouted in a weak attempt to lighten the moment.

Doc's Icon roared to life immediately when he pressed the start button. But Q's balked.

"We gotta go, Q!" Doc shouted as the boats closed to within 100 yards.

Now Doc could see the boats clearly, and he was certain they meant trouble.

"It's gotta be Guardians, Q! We gotta go now!" he shouted from his open cockpit.

"Go without me!" Q shouted back as his plane's engine refused to start.

"No way, partner!" Doc yelled back at his friend. "We came to this dance together, and we're going to leave that way … or we won't leave at all."

"We're sure not leaving just yet," Thomas said when he realized the boats were now so close, takeoff wasn't possible.

"Anybody bring a weapon?" Doc asked, hopefully.

His three companions all looked at one another, then looked at him.

"I didn't think we'd shoot the fish," Q wisecracked, trying to break the tension.

"No worries," Doc assured them. "Let's see what they want before we panic."

Moments later, the four speedboats turned off their engines and quickly drifted within feet of the small seaplanes. Each boat had four men aboard. Two of them were sleeveless, and their Guardian tattoos were easy to spot.

"Howdy!" Q shouted calmly. "We're havin' a little engine trouble. I think I'm out of gas. You got any you can spare?"

Doc stood up in the cockpit and stepped out onto his Icon's port wing. The boats had drifted together, and he could easily see all eight intruders. While he distracted them with small talk, he carefully raised the back of his fishing vest with his elbows and bent slightly forward so that his companions could see the PHASR pistol tucked into his belt at the center of his back.

"Damn! He's got Rafe's PHASR," Q whispered. "Cover your eyes!" he told the Byrnes brothers as Doc pretended to rub his eyes, then clasped his hand tightly over his eyes, yanked the PHASR out of his belt, and blasted the Guardians.

"All clear!" Doc shouted to his crew when he saw all eight Guardians were incapacitated.

Two Guardians had been standing and fell overboard when they blacked out.

"Let 'em drown!" Q shouted happily.

But Thomas and Raymon were already in the water and quickly loaded the waterlogged pair back into one of the boats.

Doc helped the brothers lash the boats together, while Q finally managed to restart the engine of his Icon.

"You two have about fifteen minutes to get these boats to my dock before this bunch starts to wake up. Q and I will be waiting for you there," Doc said as he climbed into his cockpit and began taxying for takeoff with Q close behind.

As the compact seaplanes rose into the air, Q turned on his radio and hoped Doc had too.

"Did Rafe give you that PHASR, or did you take it when he wasn't looking?" he chuckled.

"Actually, he gave it to me as a memento of our having worked together," Doc said.

"I never would have guessed the two of you had bonded, like that," Q snickered. "Far as I could tell, he pretty much wrote us both off as dumb Yankees."

"Well, I guess we did bond on some level," Doc

answered. "I've got to call the sheriff's office. Talk to you on the ground."

When the four deputies arrived, the Guardians' hands and feet were bound with zip ties.

"Sorry, but we're fresh out of handcuffs," Q told them with a shrug.

"How'd you manage to corral them with no casualties, Doc?" a deputy asked. "There's usually at least a couple when you and Q get involved with these Guardian characters. We've already called Homeland Security at Malmstrom Air Base. What do they do with these guys?"

"Don't know," Q said flatly. "Whatever they do, it ain't bad enough."

Doc noticed Thomas checking his watch as the deputies loaded the Guardians into the bus they'd brought and drove away.

"You two are headed back to Arizona today, aren't you?" he asked.

"Yep, we've shot a hole clean through our vacation time, but it was worth it," Thomas said and put an arm around his brother's shoulders. "This is the most time we've spent together in a long, long time. The last time we had together was the time we spent with you chasing more Guardians around the country. Being with you two and not getting shot at is a nice change."

"Well, we came awful close out on the water this morning," Doc reminded him, "which would have been incredibly awkward since we were unarmed. But all's well that ends well."

"I'd better call the president and make sure he's sending enough Homeland agents to stand watch over our homes until Mancini is caught."

As Doc took out his phone, it vibrated, and the presidential seal filled the screen.

"I keep tellin' ya, Doc, the man's got you bugged," Q said, only half kidding.

"I'd argue with you, Q, but you've known him a lot longer than I have," Doc chuckled.

"Good morning, Mr. President," Doc said cheerfully. "I just pulled my phone out to call you for additional Homeland support until you catch Mancini. Why did you call me?"

"Good morning, Doc!" the president boomed over the phone. "Sounds like you and the others had a little excitement this morning. So, of course, I've already called Malmstrom and made sure they're dispatching more than enough agents to you keep you folks safe. And I've got some other news for you related to your adventure on the water. Brace yourself. Jonah Baird's alive."

"Are you sure?!" Doc asked excitedly. "Do you have him in custody?"

"Not yet," the president told him. "The FBI confirmed he was photographed by an ATM camera in Manhattan. And we just got a camera shot of him buying a bus ticket to D.C. Agents waiting for him at the D.C. bus terminal. We expect to have him in custody shortly.

"Doc, I'd really like for you and the team to be here when we have him," the president said. "As usual, my personal plane is yours. It's being fueled and flight-readied and should be waiting for you in a hangar at Glacier Park when you're all ready to leave tomorrow morning."

"Roger that, Mr. President," Doc replied. "Thank you. We look forward to looking him in the face when you have him safely in custody."

"See you soon, Doc!" the president said.

"Yes, sir!" Doc said as the president ended the call.

"Did he say what I think he said?" Q asked hopefully.

"Baird's alive, and they're hunting him down as we speak," Doc said with a touch of disbelief. "The president wants us in D.C. when Baird's in custody. So we've got to alert the others and start packing. The president has Homeland headed our way to keep an eye on our homes while we're gone. So tell Marsha to pack for another D.C. shopping trip.

"We've got plenty of room on the plane for you two," Doc told the Byrnes brothers. "Do you want to be there when one of the most-wanted men of the 21st century is brought in, or do you still want to head back to Arizona and write parking tickets?"

"Whoa! That's harsh!" Thomas said defensively.

"Yeah, it was, wasn't it? I didn't mean it the way it came out," Doc said apologetically.

"I just know that the two of you were invested in catching Baird when we first met, and I figured you probably still are. That's all. And speaking for myself, I'd love to have the two of you along on this trip. I figure you've earned it."

Thomas looked at Raymon, and Raymon nodded.

"I'll make a call," Thomas said.

"Count us in!" Raymon told Doc excitedly.

About that time, Aubrey Baird awoke from her nap when she heard her uncle coming through the front door.

"My goodness, what time is it?" she asked as she wiped the sleep from her eyes. "Did I sleep the entire day away?"

"No, Dear One," the captain told her as he stood stone-still in the foyer and watched the Suburban that brought him home vanish up the street. "I left the office early."

"On your first day? Don't you feel well?" Aubrey asked him and got up from the recliner.

The captain turned from the window and silently crossed the living room to his niece.

"This photo was taken this morning," he told her as he handed her the manila envelope. "You should sit back down before you open it."

Confused and a little frightened by her uncle's demeanor, Aubrey did just that. She pulled the throw back into her lap and slowly opened the envelope as the captain sat on an ottoman beside her.

"Oh, dear God in heaven!" she gasped as he slid the photo from the envelope and saw her father's face. "He's alive, Uncle Tuck! He's alive!"

Aubrey slid from the recliner to the floor and knelt at her uncle's feet, and took his large, strong hands in hers.

"I can hardly believe it," she told her uncle with tears on her cheeks. "My prayers have been answered. Where is he, Uncle Tuck? Can we see him?"

"As soon as the FBI has him in custody," the captain told her. "But they're finding out catching him is a lot easier said than done. The president called me on the way home to tell me. The FBI has another photo of him buying a bus ticket to D.C. They intercepted the bus in Baltimore, but your father wasn't onboard. He no doubt has access to cash here in the capitol, and the best guess is he got off in Philly and is taking a cab in from there to avoid capture."

"We have to find him, Uncle Tuck!" Aubrey said desperately. "We have to find him and convince him to turn himself in."

"Your father is very cunning and resourceful, Aubrey," the captain replied. "And he no doubt has many options once he's back in the capitol. The FBI has his most obvious choices to hide under surveillance. Other than that, I don't have any idea where to begin looking for him."

"But we must find him, Uncle Tuck! We must!" she said as she broke down and cried like Tuck hadn't seen her cry since her mother and two older sisters were killed by a drunk driver when she was just seven years old.

Tuck was desperate to give his only niece a ray of hope. So he played the one card he had.

"The president also told me he's bringing in a special team to help find your father," he told her. "The members of the team have known your father for several years. If anyone can find him, they can."

"I need to meet them, Uncle Tuck," Aubrey pled. "I *must!*"

"I'm afraid that's not possible, Aubrey," the captain tried to explain. "They're an elite, top-secret team who don't even exist officially."

"I have top-secret government clearance, Uncle Tuck," she told him. "I received it while at MIT completing my doctoral thesis so that I could spend the next two years researching the federal government's aerospace data security protocols and strategies."

"How high?" the captain asked in surprise.

"The highest," she said. "Developed Vetting – Sensitive Compartmented Information."

"I'll, ugh. I'll make a call," was all the captain could think to say.

Eight minutes later, Jasper Cornwall stopped at Camilla's desk with a smile.

"You look lovely, Camilla," Cornwall said and quickly added, "as you do every day."

"Why, thank you, Jasper," Camilla gushed and blushed in response. "It's this wonderful new dress my husband got me for our anniversary."

"Congratulations! It's special alright," Cornwall replied and set a sizable gold, rope-handled gift bag on her desk. "I hope you and Mr. Renfro find this to be a little special also."

"How sweet of you!" Camilla said excitedly as she stood to peer into the bag. "Oh my goodness," she said softly as she lifted out a large Godiva Chocolate Gold Ballotin Tower wrapped bound with a fancy gold ribbon. "Thank you, Jasper!" she said as she opened the top box. "Do I have to tell Randal about this, or can I just keep it here with me?" she asked with an impish grin.

"Discretion is one of your most exceptional skills,

Camilla," Cornwall said. "So, I'll leave that decision entirely up to you."

"I'll give it some serious thought," she chuckled as Cornwall continued into the Oval. "He's having a quick lunch in his room off the Oval," she said as Cornwall let the door close behind him and headed across the Oval to the president's small private office.

"Jasper! I'm glad to see you!" the president said in a cheerful tone that surprised his chief of staff. "I can't possibly finish this chicken cordon bleu, and the chef is always disappointed if I send anything back unfinished. Help me out here, would you please?"

"Thanks, but I just had lunch, Mr. President," Cornwall replied.

"Okay, I'm ordering you to either finish it for me," the president insisted, "or I'll tell Camilla to have it wrapped and delivered to the mini-fridge in your office for tomorrow."

"I choose Option B," Cornwall said as he slouched in a chair across the table from the president. "You're in a particularly good mood, given all that's going on."

"Jasper, Bush 43 once said, 'If a problem shows up on my desk, it's because no one else can solve it.' I figure I'm most creative when I'm in a good mood. So—I work hard at staying in a good mood. Chicken cordon bleu helps a lot, which is another reason why you should finish this. You need to loosen up, my good friend! By the way, why are you here?"

"By the way, why am I here?" Cornwall echoed sarcastically. "Sometimes I feel like I should walk out the door and come back in."

"No sense of humor means something big has just happened," the president thought out loud. "What have you got for me now, Jasper?"

"Tuck just called and asked if he can bring his niece by to meet briefly with you and your Dozen when they arrive tomorrow," he said. "I told him you have your hands and head full with several critical issues— including her father's reappearance—but he insisted that I run it by you. What should I tell him?"

"Make it happen, Jasper," the president said. "I'm here all afternoon tomorrow, and Doc's crew are scheduled to arrive around noon, right?"

"Yeah, but it will stretch the meeting time, and your schedule's booked," Cornwall told him, trying to skirt the issue of getting Aubrey Baird involved in bringing her father in.

"You always manage to find me ten minutes when I need them, Jasper," the president said with obvious appreciation. "Jonah Baird once bragged to me that his daughter had earned the highest security clearance while at MIT. I confirmed that she still has it before we okayed her first visit. That means I'll be able to answer some or all of her questions, and she'll understand that details of the meeting—and its participants—are classified. So please include her, even if it means I work later than usual. Then let Tuck know when to expect a car to arrive."

"Consider it done!" Cornwall said as he rose from his chair.

"Thanks, Jasper," the president said quietly and pointed to his chicken. "I'll have Camilla get this wrapped and into your office fridge. You'll thank me; it's great!"

Doc and Connie again hosted the entire team and the Byrnes brothers for a fancy cookout luncheon gathering at the lake house. The long, rustic, solid oak dining room table that Connie and Q's wife, Marsha, found at an estate sale in the little village of Somers at the north end of the lake gave everyone plenty of elbow room. As Connie always insisted, the meal was enhanced with talk about family and friends, recent trips, and planned trips —excluding business trips.

"We're so glad that you and Tom decided to stay with us a little longer, Ray," Connie told Raymon Byrnes. "It's nice to know we'll have at least a few more days to really get to know you both. Is Montana all that different from Arizona?"

"Well, as is true of most other states, Montana's cooler, especially this time of year," Raymon told her. "But Tom and I both love the Arizona high desert region. There's really nowhere else that compares to it."

"Are there no lakes the size of Flathead there?" Marsha asked.

"Lake Pleasant, just north of Phoenix, is a pretty good-sized lake," Thomas told her. "But it's manmade. So it's no match for the natural beauty you enjoy here. Our home is made of sun and sand and stone, struggling daily to survive and managing century after century to thrive."

"You should write a book about it, Thomas," Connie told him sincerely.

"Perhaps I will someday," he told her.

Connie was thrilled when the conversation around the table throughout the meal remained firmly focused on family, friends, and fond memories of the recent past and long ago. Times like these, being among family and friends, gave her the greatest happiness. Her happiness that afternoon was so real and large it filled the lake house with warmth and fed her spirit.

This is everything she wanted her life to be about, and she savored every minute for all it was worth because she knew that sooner or later, Doc's satellite phone would vibrate, and her personal world would again collide with the world outside. She was right, of course. And not long afterward, while everyone was still gathered around the table, Doc's phone did begin to vibrate, and the real world came calling.

"Hello, Mr. President!" Doc said as cheerfully as he could. "Have you got an update?"

"I do … but honestly, it's too soon to tell whether it's good news or bad," the president told him. "Are you ready for it?"

"I was born ready," Doc said, just because he thought it sounded good.

"Jonah Baird's daughter has asked to meet the team here at the White House when you arrive tomorrow, and I've granted her request," the president said. "She's had a Sensitive Compartmented Information security clearance for a number of years, and she desperately wants to at least feel like she's involved in the effort to bring him in."

"I understand that it's your call, Mr. President," Doc said. "I also understand his daughter wanting to be involved in his capture and well-being. But my primary concern is that my team must be able to operate as efficiently and effectively as possible, without fear of interference from others who may also be involved in the search for Baird. We have our methods, and others have theirs. That said, I have no objection to Jonah's daughter being at our meeting tomorrow. In fact, we may learn a thing or two that just may serve us well."

"Excellent!" the president boomed. "I'm looking forward to the meeting. Have a safe flight, and I'll see you and the rest of my Dozen tomorrow."

"One more thing while I have you, Mr. President," Doc said. "I'd like to add Thomas and Raymon Byrnes to the list of attendees as well."

"Done!" the president boomed and ended the call saying, "See you all tomorrow."

With that call, it was clear the real world had again found the lake house, and discussions around the table shifted to the mission ahead. Connie wished it would have happened a little later in the day, but she focused on being grateful it hadn't happened sooner.

"Doc, the look on your face is the reason you'll never be my poker partner," Q said.

"I don't gamble, Q. You know that," Doc replied while he processed the call.

"Those who know your profession would beg to differ," Q wisecracked.

"I wouldn't equate what we do to playing poker," Doc said. "Our odds are better."

"I wish someone would put that in writing," Q answered and let Doc move on.

"The president has granted a request by Jonah Baird's daughter to participate in our meeting with him tomorrow," Doc announced.

"Really! Is that wise?" Jenny blurted out. "Does she have a security clearance?"

"The highest possible. Same as ours," Doc replied.

"How and when did she get it?" Louis asked next.

"At times, it seems the government gives it out for the sake of convenience," Q muttered.

"I don't think so in her case, Q," Doc said earnestly. "According to the president, Aubrey Baird was a legitimate prodigy in computer science and aerospace technologies and did some serious work for the federal government and the military to earn her way through *her* graduate studies at MIT. She definitely does not sound like a slouch."

"How come we've never heard of her before this?" Jenny asked.

"That's an excellent question for the president tomorrow," Doc told her.

"Well, whatever the reason, the president's decided to get her involved in tomorrow's meeting, and that can only mean one thing," Q concluded.

"And what would that be?" Doc asked, expecting a wisecrack he didn't get.

"Judging by the president's actions in response to all the information he has," Q guessed, "Jonah Baird, a.k.a. the Keeper, is officially considered to be back from the dead."

10

The team's swift SUV ride to the White House from Joint Base Andrews, the constant radio chatter along the route, and the rushed handoff out of the vehicles and through the west wing entrance made it clear to the team that the president wanted to begin their meeting as soon as possible. There was no fancy, relaxed welcome at the north portico this trip. Instead, they were hustled through the simple double doors of the west wing and rushed along the corridors that led to the Oval Office.

Doc knew the layout well from his time with the Secret Service, and he wondered why they didn't take the most direct route. But he quickly shrugged it off, knowing staff always has its reasons. The rush was undeniable when Camilla simply said, "Hello," and held the Oval Office door open for the team as they approached, then closed it softly behind them.

"Welcome, everybody! Doc! Q! And a special welcome

back to you both, Tom and Ray. It's good to see you all again!" the president boomed in his usual, enthusiastic greeting as he stepped from behind the Resolute.

"Hello, Mr. President, " Doc said hesitantly, and hoped he would soon understand why this meeting seemed so rushed.

"I'm sorry if this seems rushed," the president began, "but I wanted to provide you with some important background before Captain Baird and his niece join us. I've asked them to delay their arrival by fifteen, and I want to maximize the time that gives us too so that you all have some understanding of the dynamics at play in this train wreck of an episode in our continuing effort to bring Jonah Baird to justice once and for all."

"Amen to that, brother—uh, I mean, Mr. President," Q said apologetically.

"What do you already know?" the president asked to save time.

"Baird has a very smart daughter we didn't know existed until yesterday," Q replied.

"Okay, here's the skinny on Aubrey and her father," the president began as he sat back in his chair, and the team pulled up eight of the ten chairs that Camilla had set out for the meeting.

"Jonah's business success was snowballing when his wife and two oldest daughters were all killed by a drunk driver, more than two decades ago, when Aubrey was just seven years old," the president began. "Tragically, Jonah obsessed over keeping his only remaining child safe. In his fear and grief, he smothered Aubrey while trying to protect her. She was schooled at home by private tutors, had no childhood friends, and almost no contact with the outside world.

"Like her father, she is brilliant, but rebellious and soon resented her father's oppressive overprotectiveness. So, after completing her high school studies, she pressured him into handing over her inheritance, as well as what would have been her sisters' shares, walked away on her 18th birthday, and never looked back. Out of anger or spite, or both, she stopped communicating with Jonah. Not surprisingly, she is a legitimate prodigy in computer science and aerospace technologies. She earned doctorates in both at MIT by the time she was 26, and tacked on a master's degree in business, hopefully out of respect for her father, who had always hoped to someday reconcile with her and hand her the reins of his business affairs.

"In any event, she completed her undergraduate studies at MIT in just three years, so Jonah received his very first proof that she was even still alive when the school sent him a congratulatory letter announcing her graduation and acceptance into their graduate program."

"It breaks my heart to hear this," Madeleine spoke up. "I hope she came home to help find her father, rather than to simply pick at the bones of what remains of his business empire."

"Fortunately for all of us, it's the former," the president said with a slight smile. "I have no idea what her business interests might be. But I can assure you that now that we know Jonah is alive, she's desperate to help find him and bring him in. Fortunately for her, and for us, her remarkable work at MIT earned her the top-secret clearance. So we can speak freely with her."

"How freely, exactly?" Doc asked, "Does she know everything, anything, about Baird's maniacal, blood-thirsty campaign as the 'Keeper'—about his obsession to slaughter creative people around the world and memori-alize them in his grisly 'Forbidden Library'?"

"She no doubt knows bits and pieces," the president said. "There have been stories published about it, of course, some close to the truth, others so out of this world no one can possibly believe them," the president said. "But no, she does not know the whole story. No one outside of this room knows it all. That level of detail is contained in only one place on this earth, a place even more secure than the human mind, which inevitably forgets details over time."

"Where's that?" Q asked, while everyone else wondered.

"It's all in the book—all of it," the president said quietly.

"The President's Book of Secrets," Doc said just as quietly.

"A book that has never been seen by any living person, a

book that—to be totally accurate—doesn't even exist," the president said even more quietly.

"Now wait a minute, Mr. President," Q said impatiently. "You're giving me a headache. I've heard you mention the book once before. But you never said it was imaginary."

"It's not," the president replied flatly.

"Do you see?" Q exaggerated a strained expression. "This is the kinda discussion that wracks my brain."

"I'm sorry," the president said sincerely. "I'll give you the quickest possible explanation, and then we must bring Aubrey and her uncle, my new senior advisor, in and start the meeting."

That tidbit about Captain Augustus Baird made Doc's and Q's heads snap around to face one another.

"The Book is really a repository of information in tens of thousands—maybe hundreds of thousands—of files containing computer data that reside on what every cybersecurity expert we've consulted agrees is the most secure server in the world. It's in a totally secure, closely monitored room beneath the Situation Room. There is no 'Book' as you and I would think of it. When I need a printed version of a section of the Book, Jasper, my chief of staff, works with Corporal Oliver in the Situation Room to produce the only pages I need, which are burned when I'm done with them."

An LED light flashed on the president's desk just then.

"Yes, Camilla," the president pushed a button on the desk and said.

"Mr. President, Captain Baird and his niece are here," Camilla said. "May I bring them?"

"Absolutely! Please do, Camilla," the president boomed in his unique way.

Aubrey could hardly contain herself during the introductions. By the time the president was trying to explain that Doc and his team had the most in-depth knowledge about her father's habits and behaviors and that if anyone could find her father, he could, Aubrey was bursting with questions and anxiety over what she imagined to be the answers.

"Captain Holiday, I…" she blurted out.

"Call me Doc, please, Aubrey, we're all friends here," Doc assured her.

"Doc, I must find my father!" Aubrey said on the verge of tears.

"I came home from Cambridge thinking that the best I could hope for was to recover my father's body and lay him to rest," she said, wiping tears from her cheeks. "I wasted years hating him, and now that I've finally begun to understand him and the hell he's been through, a lot of which was my fault, I simply must find him. I will help you in any way I can. I know that I don't know about many things he's done. I don't care what he's done! He's my father, and he loves me deeply … and he deserves to know I love him just as deeply! So we must find him!"

Every member of the team was a little surprised by the emotion they saw on Doc's face as he thought for a moment and then told Aubrey, "We'll find him. I promise you that much."

The team was deathly silent as they strode along with Doc back to the three Suburbans that awaited them outside the west wing entrance. They were still processing Doc's surprising demeanor and his promise to Aubrey. They all knew Doc did not make promises lightly. They also knew they still did not have a clear plan, let alone a first step, regarding how to find her father … which made them all the more curious about what their next move would be.

"What are you thinking, Doc?" Q asked calmly as the SUVs began rolling toward the Willard InterContinental Hotel where they were staying.

"I'm thinking we have this afternoon to figure something out while Connie and that adventurous wife of yours thoroughly enjoy themselves at the Warner Theatre to help them not think about what we might be up to."

"I hear that!" Q said. "But what will we be up to?"

"I'm not sure yet, Q," Doc said honestly. "I'm not even sure Baird is here in D.C. No one is. But if he's here, we'll find him."

"I feel so bad for his daughter," Madeleine said. "She's

so anguished to have believed her father was dead, then to learn that he's alive, only to have him missing and being hunted like an animal."

"He kinda set that scenario in motion himself," Q reminded her.

"That doesn't make it any more bearable for her," Madeleine clarified for Q.

"Or any easier for us," Doc said. "Wait here," Doc told the driver as he climbed out of the Suburban and led the team into the lobby of the Willard InterContinental.

As the team crossed the lobby, headed for the elevators, a young voice called out from behind the reception desk.

"Doctor Holiday! Someone left a message for you about an hour ago, sir," said a fresh-faced college-age fellow wearing an impeccable hotel uniform who sprinted out from behind the huge, colorful marble kiosk and handed Doc an envelope.

Doc examined the envelope closely as the elevator doors opened. He was puzzled by it. So, of course, all seven of his companions got on the elevator with him. A little put-out about being crowded shoulder-to-shoulder, Doc delayed taking the message out of the envelope and just traded glances with everyone on board with him.

"Well, aren't you going to read it?" Jenny asked him.

"Of course I'm going to read it," Doc shot back semi-playfully. "But I don't read letters in front of people in elevators."

"Technically, it's not a letter 'cause it's not postmarked." Q played along, of course. "That's why there are only messages in bottles—and no letters. Letters that aren't postmarked are technically not letters. And yours doesn't have a postmark."

"Q! Stop!" Doc said firmly without looking up from the message.

The team all looked at the floor of the elevator and chuckled quietly.

"Please don't encourage him," Doc said in his best fake frustration.

Doc was grateful with the elevator came to a stop, and the doors opened to their floor. He quickly stepped out into the luxurious hushed hallway. The team followed close on his heels and paraded into his suite behind him, intent on knowing who the message was from and what it said. Each of them perched quickly—two on the sofa, the rest on the loveseats or armchairs. Nobody slouched. They all sat forward on the edge of their seats and gave Doc their full attention.

At that point, it had become more a game than a mystery. Annoying Doc had become more important than the note. But as they watched Doc open it and read it in a deepening silence, the game quickly dissolved into serious curiosity about what they were about to hear.

"Okay, Doc," Louis said. "We've had our fun. Who's it from, and what does it say?"

"It's kinda personal," Doc said softly without looking up from the note.

"Now I for sure want to hear it," Q couldn't stop himself from saying.

"Give him some slack, Q," Madeleine said, sensing the impact the note was having.

Doc took two steps over to Q, handed him the note, and walked to a large window that overlooked the White House grounds and the Ellipse all the way to the Washington Monument. Q read the note silently, then tipped his Stetson back on his head and read it aloud.

My Dear Dr. Holiday,

I'm here … back from the dead, some might say. My original intention was to stay just long enough to retrieve the necessary funds and dissolve into the farthest reaches of this world, never to be heard from again. And now my dear, sweet daughter Aubrey Rae is here in the hope of reuniting with me. I wish with all my heart that could happen. But the pitiful truth is, I don't have the strength of character or the courage to turn myself in and face justice.

But you, Dr. Holiday, have the courage and character of any two men. So once again, I am asking you to do the impossible. I ask that you find me and bring me to justice – or bring justice to me.

I warn you, however, it won't be easy, for though I am not brave, I will not run and I will not go down without a fight. So the challenge is set. Find me, defeat me and seal the fate I deserve.

With all my respect and admiration,

Jonah Baird (The Keeper)

"What a bizarre way to taunt you," Jenny said.

"I don't know, Jenny," Louis told his wife. "He sounds genuinely conflicted."

"It sounds to me like an attempt at 'Suicide by Cop,'" Raymon remarked.

"Well, Doc," Q said, "It sounds like your first-ever request for an assisted suicide."

"He definitely sounds more dangerous than ever to me," Madeleine remarked.

"Especially with who-knows-how-many Guardians around him," Noah added.

"I fear we'll find out how many before this is over," Doc sighed, staring out the window. "Baird doesn't seem to know Mancini's searching for his money, which makes me believe the Guardians allied with Mancini are a separate threat. We may be fighting two enemies, not one."

"I say let the F.B.I. worry about Mancini and his Juggalo bunch," Q said.

"I'd be happy to," Doc replied. "But Mancini might find it hard to overlook the fact that we kept him from taking

Baird's gold and silver stockpile just a few blocks from here. We need to get this note to the White House. Aubrey Baird needs to know her father has set the stage for the most dangerous of cat and mouse games, and we're playing for keeps. So it will either end well, and she'll have the time with her father she's hoping for, or it will end badly, and his time will run out altogether.

"She needs to see this note. So does the president. We have to get it to the White House, and then go to work," Doc said soberly.

"Finally!" Q said just loud enough to ensure Doc heard it.

Each member of the team felt the beginnings of an adrenalin rush as they headed back to the SUVs with Doc. Halfway through the lobby of the hotel, Doc suddenly pivoted in search of surveillance cameras. Then he dashed over the young man behind the reservation desk who had handed him Baird's note earlier.

"Does the hotel have surveillance cameras here in the lobby?" Doc asked the young man.

"Yes, sir," the man replied matter-of-factly. "You're being photographed as we speak."

"How are the images being captured?" Thomas Byrnes said abruptly as he stepped up to the desk and flashed his F.B.I. identification.

"On our server in the room behind me," the young man told them.

"I'd like a download of the image of whoever left this note for Dr. Holiday," Thomas said. "Will you please cooperate with this investigation and give me a copy on a flash drive?"

"Um—of course," the young man replied and quickly did what Thomas asked.

"Thank you, son," Thomas said genuinely. "The Bureau appreciates your cooperation."

"That wasn't exactly legal," Q told Thomas what they both already knew.

"Not at all," Thomas said with a wily grin as he dropped the flash drive into his pocket.

"Thanks, Tom," Doc interrupted to say to Thomas. "I want the White House to have a copy for the complete record of this mission."

"Thought so," Thomas simply answered and followed Doc and the rest of the team out to the waiting SUVs.

As the team got back into the gleaming Suburbans, Doc speed-dialed Jasper Cornwall.

"Hello, Doc!" Cornwall said cheerfully. "What's up?"

"I'm headed your way with a note I just received from Jonah Baird and a photo of him leaving it at the Willard. I'd appreciate your getting both items to the president so he can share them with Baird's daughter and then do with it as he sees fit."

"I can do that, of course," Cornwall said. "He's in the Situation Room with her and Tuck at the moment. But I'll make sure he gets them pronto. Where are you headed?"

"We're going to make a quick stop at the 'Citadel' and then we're going hunting," Doc said flatly.

"Well, good luck, be careful, and keep your powder dry," Cornwall said and hung up.

Nine minutes later, Corporal Chance Oliver paused, speaking to the president mid-sentence when the indicator light flashed as Cornwall pushed the elevator "Down" button on his way to the Situation Room. Chance looked at the live image on the screen of Cornwall in the elevator and finished his sentence as the elevator doors opened, and Cornwall stepped into the Situation Room.

"Welcome, Jasper!" Chance told him and quickly spotted the note and flash drive in a Ziplock bag he had in his left hand. "What do you have for us today?"

"Hello, Chance," Cornwall replied. "Hello to you too, Aubrey, Tuck!" he added.

"What do have for us, Jasper?" the president asked.

"Something interesting, I'm sure," his chief of staff replied and handed him the bag.

The president quickly opened it while Cornwall explained, "Doc just dropped these off. He told me he just received the note that Baird left for him, and he wants you and Aubrey to see it. The flash drive contains a photo of Baird handing the note to staff at the Willard. It's our proof he's alive."

"Can we see the photo, please?" Aubrey desperately asked.

"Sure," Chance said and inserted the flash drive into the port on his keyboard and hit a few keys to send the image to the 120-inch screen on the wall in front of them.

"Is that him?" Chance asked as he squinted at the image of an apparently older man wearing a long, black leather trench coat and a wide-brim Wesley fedora that obscured his face.

"I really can't tell if that's your father," the president told Aubrey as they all squinted.

"Me either," Aubrey replied as she stepped closer to the screen.

"Me either," Tuck agreed.

"Chance, call the Willard and get all the photos they have of this fellow. We need a better look, and then we need to upload everything to the 'President's Dozen' file on Pinnacle, " the president said, then opened the note and began reading.

"Will do, Mr. President," Chance said and went to his desk to make the call.

"What's the note say?" Aubrey asked the president.

"We better move into a side room," he told her and allowed her to lead the way to the nearest open door.

Inside the room, the president leaned against the metal table and handed Aubrey the note. As she read it, a tear ran down her left cheek. Soon, another ran down her right cheek, and the president slowly moved toward her, fearing her emotions might overwhelm her. When she began to sob, Tuck enfolded her in his arms and let her cry into his chest.

"He sounds so desperately sad," she said through her tears. "He's been through so much loss, so much hurt … and all I've ever done is add to it. I feel so ashamed," she sobbed.

"Don't be so hard on yourself, dear one," Tuck told her. "His mention of you is the best part of the note. He loves you very much, and I'm sure he's very pleased to know you've come looking for him."

"He probably thinks I've just come back for more money," Aubrey sobbed and leaned on to her uncle.

"I don't believe that for a minute," Tuck told her. "And I'm sure your father sees your return as an answer to a prayer."

"I wish I could believe that," Aubrey sobbed.

"The last thing your father told me during his visit while I was getting the help I needed was that the only prayer he was still praying was for you to come home to him," Tuck said. "And my most vivid memory of that remark is that he said 'No matter the reason' three times."

"We have to find him, Uncle Tuck!" Aubrey said, "We just have to!"

"We know your father's here now," Tuck assured her. "And Doc and his team are looking for him. Believe me, there's no one better for the job."

"I pray you're right, Uncle Tuck," Aubrey said softly and gave the note back to the president with a brave smile. "Thank you for caring about my father," she told him.

"He's a very good man with very deep troubles," the president told her gently. "But most of all, he's a good friend of many years. During those years, your father gave me a lot of priceless advice about business and about life. I owe him much. Bringing him in safely and reuniting the two of you is the least I can do to repay him."

The LED in the center of the table flashed just them.

"Looks like Chance wants to update us," the president said.

Tuck opened the door, and Chance bolted in and closed the door firmly behind him.

"The Willard emailed me three more shots of the guy in

the hat, but I still can't swear it's Jonah Baird," he told the president.

"Let's take a look," the president said and led the group back into the Situation Room.

Before telling the president, Chance put the new photos on the big screen side by side.

"See what I mean?" he asked the trio.

"It's that damned hat he's wearing," Tuck said in frustration.

"Which makes these photos awful suspicious," Chance added.

"How so?" the president asked.

"Well, there isn't much danger of anyone on the street or the hotel recognizing Baird," he explained. "Speaking of the street, I got another shot of him the D.C. police captured on a street cam at 4th Street N.W and Pennsylvania, just east of the hotel. The hat obscures his face on that one too. I couldn't even run it through our FR software. So I'm suspicious of that hat."

"Well, save the JPGs to a file named 'Suspicious' and upload this note too, please," the president said. "And Chance, have you yet begun printing a hard copy of that file yet?"

"Not yet, sir," Chance said warily. "We've got the premium paper stock on order. Printing will begin the moment we get it in."

"Well, print it out on whatever paper you have in the meantime, then make the switch when you have the other paper," the president said simply and turned his attention back to Aubrey and Tuck.

"You mean you don't routinely print a hard copy of your uploaded data?" Aubrey asked.

"The previous administration stopped the practice," the president told her.

"Seriously?" she shot back at Chance and the president in disbelief. "How is the Book preserved if the power goes out, or the server crashes, or a dozen other things go wrong?"

"Our power never goes out," Chance told her. "We've got back-up generators. And Pinnacle is really two identical servers that continually back one another up."

"Well, that at least addresses the security of the data that's already uploaded," Aubrey said. "But it doesn't address the authenticity and veracity of data that's destined to be uploaded."

"Our methods are a huge improvement over those of the past," Chance said defensively.

"I'm not questioning your methods, Chance," Aubrey assured him. "I'm just curious about the information the world has romantically labeled, the 'President's Book of Secrets.'"

"I can tell you security and integrity were vastly

improved when President Prescott promoted me to director and gave me free rein to tighten the ship," Chance boasted. "Before, the networked system from their work computers using virtual private network software limited each of them to using a particular workstation. They created and marshaled intel files into a queue for eventual upload to Pinnacle with little oversight into their creation or modification, and they could designate groups of users they gave permission to view and edit the in the queue. So, in addition to the potential abuses the process presented to matters surrounding file creation and integrity, we discovered prior abuses of 'over-classifying' data records," Chance added.

"What do you mean?" Aubrey pressed him for details.

"Members of that small army of users sometimes blocked access to intel that could be politically embarrassing or damaging to a president, such as recordings of phone calls made to foreign heads of state or other foreign officials by parking them in the queue. There was no rule prohibiting such parking of files with a lower-level classification into the queue merely to take advantage of its tighter access restrictions."

"So in the midst of all that handing-off of files, no one preserved a hard copy of their content—the 'one true copy' of the official record in its original, unaltered state?"

"Nope!" Chance shot back to her.

"That's worse than a recipe for abuse—it was an implicit invitation!" Aubrey told him.

"Yep!" Chance flatly agreed.

"It's also ancient history now," the president interrupted the conversation. "Chance, please upload Jonah's note, and archive the original."

"Now that's how it should be done," Aubrey said approvingly.

"Which is exactly why we now do it," the president replied with a smile. "Of course, Chance and his team have a mountain range of back documents to print out and archive in hard copy. But they will eventually get it caught up. Let's go back up to the Oval, and I'll check in with Doc by phone before the two of you leave."

The president got an update from Doc and was ending the call when an LED flashed on the inner edge of the president's side of the Resolute. He picked up a direct line to Chance in the Situation Room and said simply, "What's up?"

"I think you should come back down right away," Chance said as calmly as he could.

"Tuck, I'll trust you to get your delightful—and most helpful—niece home," the president said. "See you in the morning."

As Aubrey and her uncle exited the Oval, the elevator doors had already closed, and the president presented

his right palm and retina to the scanner and pressed the
" button.

"Tell me you were kidding," the president said as the
elevator door opened to Chance.

"I wish I could," Chance said solemnly. "We seem to
have a problem."

"Chance, you've never called me down here when we've
'seemed' to have a problem before," the president noted
as Chance led him into the same soundproof side room
were just minutes before, Chance had explained to
Aubrey how secure the data was on Pinnacle.

"Tell me the news in a nutshell," the president said. "I
have a meeting in five minutes."

"Okay," Chance said and took a deep breath. "I easily
uploaded the four JPG files and saved them to a new file
marked 'Suspicious' as soon as you directed me to. I
created that file within the 'President's Dozen' file that's
been part of the Book since the day you had Navy
SEALs assist Doc and his team on the coast of Israel
more than three years ago—just as you directed me to
do back then. And it's been there ever since … until it
all vanished about ten minutes ago."

"Okay, so the 'President's Dozen' file is missing?" the
president asked hopefully.

"No, sir!" Chance said in panic and frustration. "The
entire 'Book of Secrets' is gone!"

The president stood rock-still and stone-silent for five eye blinks and processed what he'd just heard.

"Define 'gone,'" the president said, hoping he misunderstood Chance's statement.

"Absent! Disappeared! Vanished! Missing! Disparu! Desaparcido! Mancante!" Chance said, almost breathless.

"Okay, I get it," the president said. "But you're sure it was here earlier today, right?"

"Absolutely!" Chance said in a defensive tone.

"So where could it be?" the president asked, assuming he'd get a reasonable answer.

"I have no idea!" Chance said bluntly. "Pinnacle's not networked. So it wasn't hacked. I've checked the metadata and the closed-circuit camera videos thoroughly, twice each, before I panicked … uh … I mean, before I summoned you," Chance assured the president. "No one but me has been anywhere near Pinnacle all day. Let alone during the past hour."

"And the Book is completely gone?" the president asked, one more time for clarity.

"It's completely gone!" Chance confirmed yet again.

"That's impossible!" the president said flatly.

"You're right," Chance told him. "It's impossible. But it's happened."

11

THE HEAD OF THE SNAKE

The building Doc had dubbed the "Citadel" was once a decrepit studio apartment above a threadbare café on the Potomac River's north bank, near the Francis Scott Key Memorial Bridge. But soon after Doc banked the head-spinning fee Jonah Baird paid him for finding the lost treasure of the Knights Templar, he bought the building and transformed it into a highly secure, high-tech hideout where he could comfortably withdraw from the world whenever he wanted.

Doc soon began stockpiling an extensive collection of impressive weapons there as well, most of which he discovered during subsequent missions overseas and immediately imported. There were also a surprising number of classified military prototypes, such as the PHASR pistol Rafe, Madeleine's French Foreign Legionnaire brother, gave him as a memento of their working together on what became known as the mission to find the "Nostradamus Scrolls."

Doc seldom visited the state-of-the-art high-tech fortress now that he and Connie had put down deep roots in Montana. But it still served him well as a secret, highly secure armory where he could stockpile powerful, exotic weapons far-removed from the normal life he and Connie were establishing in their grand fieldstone and log home, peacefully overlooking Flathead Lake, 3,000 miles away in the northern reaches of the Rocky Mountains.

Doc had purposely left the D.C. structure's exterior untouched. To passersby, it was just another ramshackle building being neglected on the outskirts of D.C. But inside, the Citadel's interior was a masterpiece: 20,000 square feet of finely finished teak wood, mahogany, industrial stainless steel, carbon fiber, and bulletproof, two-way glass. Doc had also installed industry-leading security and fire-suppression systems, powered by a new, commercial-grade water line and underground electrical service.

The few times Doc had been there since the transformation was completed, he smiled the whole time he was there, fondly recalling days that now seemed a lifetime ago when he hobbled around in severe pain inside 400 square feet of noisy, leaky, musty, crumbling plywood, fiberboard, and linoleum. All that changed when he met Jonah Baird, who introduced himself as the "Keeper" and hired Doc for the first of his legendary missions and paid him a fee beyond his wildest dreams for finding the long-lost Templar treasure.

In those days, Doc and his team had not yet earned the nickname the "President's Dozen." He had only Q, Madeleine, and Noah—and of course, his best friend, Mountain Matua, who gave his life for that first mission. In those days, Madeleine and Noah were dating but soon married. The team expanded to six when Connie's kindness to strangers resulted in her and Doc meeting Jenny and Louis Danforth, married Marines of extraordinary valor and skills.

After the success of a second mission, the resident fondly referred to the six-member team as the "President's Dozen," saying their record of success proved they each had enough courage and ability for two warriors. Though their existence was highly classified, the nickname quickly caught on throughout the president's staff. Doc always smiled his biggest smile when he thought of the times the president insisted on including the contributions of Connie and Q's wife, Marsha, when thanking and praising the team. Like the president, Doc knew their roles were as critical as they were unofficial, and he appreciated the president acknowledging them.

But this time, on what Doc was determined would be the team's final mission, he was grateful Connie and Marsha were not involved. He appreciated knowing the two of them were spending the afternoon enjoying each other's company and a great show at the Warner Theatre, topped off with a great meal at the Columbia

Square Lounge. They'd earned it on missions past. Now he was happy to have them out of harm's way while he and the team faced the mission of their lives: Capturing the Keeper, Jonah Baird, which, as far as Doc could tell, would require them to first fight their way past a new foe named Mancini, who had a score to settle with the team and apparently also wanted the Keeper out of circulation, at least—and dead, at worst.

Until that afternoon, the other team members didn't know the "Citadel" existed. Unaware of its former condition, they wondered why Doc had apparently gone to such lengths disguising the building's exterior, never guessing that the outside, in fact, was the true history of the structure. While they wandered around the first floor and then the second, they marveled at the obvious craftsmanship and high-end materials all around them. Doc pushed a button concealed behind a tile in a mosaic wall hanging, and the middle three sections of a massive wall-length bookcase slid four feet forward to reveal the room containing his vast weapons collection.

"Well, I'll be!" Q said with eyes open wide in wonder as he strode into the room behind Doc. "What else don't I know about you after all this time, Doc?" he asked with a sly grin.

"Besides this, not much else," Doc said with a shrug and sly grin of his own. "Look around, people," he told the team. "If you see something you think you might be able to use to our benefit in the fight of our lives, grab it. I have plenty of ammo for everything you see here."

They each already had their usual side arms with them. Doc wore his faithful Wilson Combat X9 1911 and stuck his PHASR pistol in a thigh pocket of his cargo pants. Q was carrying his 9mm Kriss Vector II. Of course, Madeleine wore her new semi-automatic Bursa Thunder 380. Jenny and Louis both were carrying their Marine-issued 9mm SIG M18s. That left Noah, who was never quite comfortable carrying a pistol. Doc caught him looking over a pair of Chinese broadswords with back strap sheaths that also carried an 18-inch sword.

"I'll wear one if you will," Doc told the black Swiss former European HEMA champion.

"You've got a deal!" Noah said excitedly and quickly slipped on the back strap sheath.

Doc followed suit and then picked up and loaded a 26-round automatic XRail shotgun.

"I want everyone to carry one of these as well," Doc said, hefting the XRail. "And strap on an ammo belt with another 26 shells, just for safety's sake."

"I'd say we will be able to stop just about anybody or anything in its tracks," Q said. "Including an elephant stampede."

"That's precisely the idea, Q," Doc assured him. "This time is for keeps. I intend to bring Baird in alive if possible, or dead if necessary."

"Yeah, well, be sure to save some of your ammo for that

Mancini character," Q said. "He's bound to be in the mix somewhere. And I suspect he'll be gunning for Baird as much as he will be for us."

"That'll be just fine with me," Doc said. "I'm a firm believer in divide and conquer. If Mancini's already done the dividing, I say all the better."

"Well, now that we're all dressed up, do we know where we're going?" Jenny asked as she cinched her ammo belt over a shoulder and across her chest.

"I'm interested in hearing how we're going to get wherever we're going armed the way we are," Q chuckled. "We might attract a little attention walking down the street or taking a bus, and I doubt an Uber driver will even let us near the vehicle."

"Public transportation won't be necessary," Doc told them.

Doc led them back down to the first floor and through another hidden door to the garage.

"HOLY SHIT! Oh, please excuse me, ladies." Q said in mock contriteness as the motion sensors activated the overhead lights and illuminated a monstrous, hulking, armored, black Conquest Knight XV. "What sort of gas mileage does this thing get?"

"You have to ask, you can't afford one," Doc assured him.

"A while back when we trashed four of these on your

front lawn in Montana, I thought you said you weren't in the market for one," Noah noted.

"That's when I thought we were all about to retire," Doc replied. "You see how that worked out, don't ya'? You're driving," Doc added and tossed Noah the keys. "The garage door opener's on the visor. All aboard!" Doc yelled as he climbed into a second-row seat behind Noah.

Noah brought the 14,000-pound beast to life as the rest of the team climbed aboard and strapped into the contoured high-back bucket seats.

"Remember Noah, this monster can hit 100 miles per hour, but it weighs seven tons and doesn't exactly stop on a dime," Doc said with a hand on Noah's shoulder. "The armor plating on this bad boy is three inches thick. The glass is six inches thick. Inside this rolling fortress is the safest place to be. There are gun ports everywhere you look. This is the safest place to be."

"But where are we going?" Madeleine asked from the other front seat as the garage door slowly opened, and Noah put the Conquest into gear.

"We're going to need to drive around a bit while I think about whether a couple of things I've had in the back of my mind add up," Doc said, knowing he didn't sound very assuring.

"Take the Key Bridge across the river," Q told Noah. "What the heck. Might as well enjoy the Virginia scenery while Doc thinks about which way we should really go."

Noah took the bridge and headed south along the river on the Washington Memorial Parkway. The massive armored vehicle rolled by Theodore Roosevelt Island. It was a beautiful ride while it lasted.

"I've got a hunch I really have to explore," Doc finally said. "Get us over to St. John's Church again, Noah."

"Oh no, Doc," Q moaned. "You don't really think there's still something worth beating the bushes for under the church, do ya … not after all the hell we've raised there?"

"Baird doesn't know about that, Q," Doc said. "All he knows is that he stashed around $80 million in gold and silver there. There's a chance he'll show up with the crew of Guardians he'll need to help him haul some or all of it out. If and when he does, I want to be there,"

"'If' and 'when' are mighty big words in situations like this, Doc," Q said doubtfully.

"Granted—it's just a hunch Q, not a guarantee," Doc shot back as he looked at the road ahead over Noah's right shoulder. "But we don't have anything else to go on at the moment. Take the Teddy Roosevelt Bridge back over the river into D.C.," he told Noah.

"If your hunch is what I think it is, Doc," Madeleine chimed-in, "I'd say don't underestimate it. You just might be on to something."

"Let's talk about it, Madeleine," Doc said enthusiastically. "Remember the tunnel beneath the Templar stronghold in Acre, Israel?" he asked her.

"Of course," she replied with a broad, knowing smile as she surmised Doc's thoughts.

"Do you also remember how you brilliantly surmised that the knights had originally used the tunnel, not for escapes, but to bring treasure up from the harbor to the fortress?" Doc asked.

"That was brilliant, wasn't it?" Madeleine said with a smile. "So keep going, Doc. What are you thinking?"

"I'm thinking about how in the world Baird got $80 million in gold and silver beneath St. John's Church without causing a single eyebrow to go up," Doc continued.

"Are you thinking that perhaps there's a tunnel that runs from the church to some other location?" she asked with a now-impish smile.

"I believe there must be," he answered. "Before I ever set foot in St. John's, I had an intriguing encounter just two blocks away, up H Street. A Mr. Oliver invited me to stop by Quest Publishing to discuss publication of an autobiography I had begun writing."

"You were writing an autobiography before our first mission together?" Q asked in amazement. "Where can I buy a copy?"

"You're not funny, Q," Doc replied, eager to continue his conversation with Madeleine. "Does the name Oliver ring any bells with you?" he asked Madeleine.

"Oliver … Oliver," Madeleine murmured while she thought about it. "The corporal in the Situation Room is named Chance Oliver!"

"Bingo!" Doc said. "I never actually met the mysterious Mr. Oliver, but he provided the key I needed to enter St. John's basement. So right now, my gut is telling me two things: First, the elusive Mr. Oliver, who we know is linked to Jonah Baird, could also have some connection with Chance Oliver that results in information from the Situation Room reaching Baird. Second, there must be another access point to Baird's chamber under St. John's, which enables him to transport treasure and people to and from the church property. My best guess is that the other end of the tunnel is at Quest Publishing."

"Doc, D.C. sits atop a massive maze of tunnels," Madeleine finally said. "It's been my personal research project for years since I learned of it in college. The first were simple steam tunnels, dug during the Civil War era. Later, high-security tunnels were added to safely transport money between government buildings. Then pedestrian tunnels were dug to ease travel for the exploding number of government employees in bad weather. And of course, the subway system was eventually added. There are now hundreds of miles of tunnels of every kind."

"So a man with money could conceivably add one or

two of his own to the mix and maximize the existing system for his personal benefit." Doc did the math out loud.

"Conceivably!" Madeleine said excitedly.

"Well, let's quit theorizin' and check it out," Q said flatly. "Where'd you say Quest Publishing is?"

"It's just a few steps from the intersection of H Street and 17th Street," Doc said.

"That will have to be a long tunnel," Q said doubtfully.

"Yeah, about the length of the one the Knights Templar dug by hand—700 years ago," Doc made his point.

Q rarely fell silent for a couple of blocks, processing Doc's hunches.

"Drop me off at Quest Publishing," he finally said to Noah.

"What are you thinkin', Q?" Doc asked warily, concerned about the element of surprise.

"I'm going to be your literary agent for a few minutes to see if Mr. Oliver will surface and give me the time of day," Q replied.

Noah slowly rolled the Conquest past the address a couple of minutes later.

"Pull over and let me out," Q said soberly as he made sure the clip of his 9mm was fully loaded, then slipped it back into its holster under his vest.

"Remember, Q, that's a lethal weapon, not a business card," Doc said ominously.

"Have a little faith in me, would ya, Doc?" Q sighed, with exaggerated exasperation.

"I have a great deal of faith in you, Q," Doc replied. "I just know that you're sometimes less tolerant of deception than at other times. And I don't know which of those times this is."

"Well, we're about to find out," Q said as he opened the rear door of the Conquest.

"Wait," Madeleine suddenly said. "I'll go. I need to use the bathroom anyway."

"What?" Q said with a hint of offense. "You think you can be more persuasive than a 9mm semi-automatic?"

"I know I can be a lot less alarming," she replied while she quickly adjusted her hair using the rearview mirror.

"I second the motion," Doc interjected, and Madeleine quickly exited the SUV. "His offices are at the end of the long hallway you'll find inside. Just follow the signs."

In a moment, Madeleine disappeared beyond the nondescript office building's brass double doors, walking her most feminine walk.

"This may shock you, Q," Doc said. "But your 9mm is no match for feminine wiles."

"You may have a valid point there," Q murmured as he

squinted to see Madeleine walking inside across the lobby.

Just as Doc had three years earlier, Madeleine followed the ornate wall signs down a labyrinth of marble-lined hallways, deep into the building. When she came to a door marked Quest Publishing, she stood for a moment, listened to the silence on the other side, and unbuttoned two more buttons on the front of her blouse. Then she slowly opened the door and strode into the silence. Inside, Madeleine found the same broad, empty counter of polished wood and marble that had greeted Doc. The large, shiny brass bell was still there. So was the sign beside it that read, *Please ring bell for service.* So she rang it.

"Can I help you?" asked the same older gentleman in the same elegant navy-blue suit who greeted Doc. He'd suddenly appeared from some room or other behind the counter.

"Hello, my name is Vanessa Walker," Madeleine lied. "I am Dr. John Henry Holiday's literary agent, and I'm hoping to have a few moments with Mr. Oliver."

"I'm pleased to meet you, Ms. Walker," the gentleman said. "My name is Everett Johns, and I regret having to tell you that it won't be possible to meet with Mr. Oliver without an appointment. He is an extremely busy man. But I'll be happy to take a message and your card and make sure that he gets them. I'm afraid that's the best I can do under the circumstances."

"Oh, please forgive me for not phoning first to request

an appointment, but I just happened to be in town from New York, and I realized that although speaking to Mr. Oliver was one of the tasks I hoped to accomplish while here, I neglected to call ahead. It's really quite embarrassing, but I'm afraid I also neglected to bring along my business cards. Oh, I do hope he can spare a few moments to speak with me."

"I see. Please wait here. I'll be right back," the gentleman said and disappeared into the room behind the counter.

Madeleine strained to hear anything the mysterious Mr. Oliver might say in response to her plea, but all she heard was silence. She guessed Mr. Oliver wasn't receptive to her plea. So she braced herself for an abrupt rejection when Mr. Johns returned to the counter.

"What exactly is the nature of your business again, Ms. Walker?" he asked awkwardly. That wasn't a question she had prepared an answer for. So she made it up as she went along.

"Dr. Holiday has finally completed his autobiography and is most interested in exploring publishing arrangements as Mr. Oliver proposed some time ago," she told him.

"Well, Mr. Oliver asked me to tell you that Quest Publishing no longer deals in non-fiction, particularly biographies and autobiographies," Mr. Johns told her flatly and handed her an expensive-looking embossed business card. "But he also asked me to tell you that if you would be kind enough to mail the manuscript to his attention at this address, he will be happy to refer and recommend Dr. Holiday's work to an appropriate publishing house.

"Thank you for thinking of Quest Publishing and taking time out of what I am sure is a very busy schedule to stop in and see us. However, should you ever wish to meet with Mr. Oliver again, please request an appointment in advance. Good day, Ms. Walker," he said curtly.

"Umm … thank you for all your help, Mr. Johns," Madeleine stammered. "Good day."

She almost broke into a run in her rush to get back to the SUV. Doc saw her coming, leaned over the front passenger seat, and opened her door as she approached. She hopped in with a sigh of relief.

"If that's a legitimate publishing house, I'm a Sumo wrestler," she told the team and handed the business card to Doc. "You haven't even finished your autobiography, and you already have your first rejection … but I doubt it's very motivating. That place is creepy!"

"Did you meet Mr. Oliver?" Doc asked anxiously.

"Nope," Madeleine told him. "At least, I don't think so."

"Maybe you shoulda let me go in," Q said sarcastically.

"What do you mean, Madeleine?" Doc asked, ignoring Q completely.

"I just got the feeling that the guy who comes to the

counter is the only guy there—ever," she told Doc. "If you ask me, the place is just a front, and Mr. Johns is a modern-day watchman, a 21st century Julienne Artimus LaDevereux."

"I got the same feeling when I walked in, three years ago," Doc agreed.

"I'm lost," Louis grumbled in the back seat. "Who's Julienne Artimus LaDevereux?"

"A mysterious memory from a mission long ago … literally," Q told him. "When she has more time, Madeleine can bring you up to speed on our old friend, LaDevereux. And I do mean old. But be sure to have your wildest imagination with you when she tells you the story."

"So, what's really going on in there?" Noah asked his wife.

"I don't think we can be sure," Madeleine said with frustration. "Frankly, 'Mr. Oliver' could merely be a code name that tips off Mr. Johns when people with government connections come around. It's all very fishy—fishy enough to be a gateway to the chamber under the church as you suspect, Doc. But I fear the only way we'll know for sure is to head back down to St. John's, find the tunnel we know must be there, and see where it takes us."

"Sounds like a crapshoot to me, folks," Q said. "And what will we have to show for it even if your hunch is right, Doc? What good is a tunnel if it doesn't lead us to Baird—or at least some of his Guardians who might tell us where he is?"

"And what if we don't find a tunnel?" Doc asked, momentarily drawn into Q's cynicism.

"Well, we'll for sure never find it sitting here," Jenny said anxiously.

"Roger that!" Doc replied loudly. "If there is a tunnel and the rats come running out at this end, we will need four of you here to round them up."

"But that leaves only two of us to go into the basement, which could either be empty ... or a den of vipers," Madeleine realized. " So what are ya thinkin', Doc? Are we going to do 'Paper, Rock, Scissors,' or are you going to decide who goes to the head of the snake and forces whoever's there out of the tunnel ... if there is one?"

"That'll be Q and me," Doc said emphatically. "The rest of you will cover the front and back of Quest Publishing in case those vipers you mentioned come slithering out."

"There's no way we can hang around outside without attracting a lot of attention," Jenny said. "We should probably have at least two large cargo vans."

"You're right, Jenny," Doc agreed. "We can rent two not far from here. You and Louis will take one. Madeleine, you and Noah will take the other. Park them out of the way, but close enough to corral anyone who comes out of the building."

"Q and I will take the Conquest to St. John's," Doc continued.

"I'm drivin'!" Q interrupted with his best "excited little boy" voice.

"If we find Guardians and a tunnel," Doc continued, ignoring Q, "we'll drive them out, and one of you can take us back to the Conquest when the smoke clears and the shooting stops. I'll tip the president to what we're up to and make sure we have Homeland Security nearby to help us keep this under control at your end."

"Speaking of Homeland Security," Q interjected, "tell me again why we don't just let them handle this entire matter, Doc."

"It all boils down to Jonah Baird, Q," Doc said flatly. "The president has a history with him, but he's keenly aware of the death and destruction Baird's capable of. The president knows we have a history with Baird too. And he hopes we'll be able to take Baird with a minimum of force while attracting a minimum of attention. That's a tall order here in D.C."

"Too tall, if you ask me," Q replied. "But I know, you haven't asked me."

Forty-five minutes later, the President's Dozen was back on H Street with two large cargo vans. Louis and Jenny sat in the van parked on the curb in front of Quest

Publishing. Madeleine and Noah sat in the second van, parked in a small parking area at the rear of the building. If Guardians exited the building, one couple or the other would have the drop on them before the door they came out of could close.

Minutes later, Q slowly pulled the Conquest to the curb on the H Street side of St. John's.

"You know it's impossible not to attract attention in this beast, right?" Q asked rhetorically.

"I'm just asking you to help me keep as low a profile as we can," Doc reminded Q. "Don't take undue risks, and don't fire a weapon in the church unless it's absolutely necessary. Do your best, Q—like you always do," Doc said flatly. "I'm going in first to scope the place out and figure the best way for us to do this. We really don't want anyone seeing us packing XRail shotguns through the church if we can avoid it."

"It would clear the place fast," Q chuckled. "But I guess your way makes more sense."

"I'm glad you think so," Doc sighed. "Wait here," he said simply.

When the sidewalk was empty, Doc exited the Conquest with the XRail slung over his right shoulder and the handle of his broadsword visible over his left. He silently mounted the few stone steps to the church's side entrance and slowly opened it. No one but Q saw Doc disappear into the church. The former Navy SEAL made no sound as he peered into the sanctuary and saw no one there. Thrilled, Doc stuck his head out the side entrance and signaled Q to join him. From there, reaching the basement was a breeze. But as they descended the stairs, they heard voices echoing off the concrete walls.

"We've looked for hours," one voice said. "If gold and silver were here, we would've found it by now."

"Just keep looking," a second voice ordered. "The Keeper will be here sometime this afternoon, and we need to find the metals before he arrives."

"But you gotta understand," the first voice said anxiously, "if the Keeper knows Lord Mancini wants to kill him, he may never show up here. Well, there'll be hell to pay if we're empty-handed when the Keeper shows up. So get off your ass and help us look for it!"

Q signaled Doc to switch on his two-way radio.

"Do you want to hole up until the Keeper shows or corral the snakes now?" he whispered over the radio.

"Get comfortable and let's see what happens," Doc answered. "Noah, are you hearing this?" he asked over the radio, hoping the signal was making it out of the basement.

"Loud and clear, Doc," Noah replied.

"Us too," Jenny checked in.

"We'll give Baird an hour to show up," Doc told them.

"If he doesn't—or this bunch starts to leave—we'll move on them. Until then, stand by."

"Aye, aye, Doc," Louis answered.

"Understood," Noah said. "Keep us posted."

"Get comfortable, Q," Doc said softly and found a comfortable spot behind a wide pillar.

A half-hour later, Doc and Q suddenly felt a rush of fresh air from behind them. Someone was coming downstairs.

"Steady!" Doc whispered over the radio.

Q took the safeties off his 9mm and the deadly XRail.

"Can you see who's coming down the stairs?" Q asked quietly over the radio.

"I see a small crowd," Doc whispered back.

"More Guardians?" Q wondered aloud.

"Yeah, and this bunch are all in Juggalo makeup and hoods," Doc told him.

"What?" Q asked urgently.

"Stand by, folks, I believe things are about to get interesting."

"And loud!" Q added.

From his hiding place, Doc counted 23 hooded figures as they descended the stairs. In the dim light, he thought he saw several of them wearing silver rings like the one that sparked this mission in the first place.

"This has to be Mancini's bunch," Doc whispered. "There's 23 of them, and things are about to get very interesting."

12

THE WORST FORM OF VENGEANCE

The biggest of the bunch, around 6'10" and 260 pounds, boldly led them down the stairs. He didn't seem worried that the Guardians who were already there would know that he and his crew had arrived. In fact, he was about to make sure they knew. He paused on the third step from the bottom, and the gang behind him stopped immediately. Chest out, shoulders back, he lowered his hood and exposed a gigantic bald head and bold Juggalo makeup. The overhead lights glinted off the oversized sterling silver Death Ring on his left hand. He looked more like a front man for a shock-rock, glam-metal band than the merciless killer he was.

"Well, if it ain't Mancini," one of the Guardians searching the basement said.

"Lord Mancini to you!" Mancini loudly demanded.

"You're no lord to us, Mancini," the Guardian replied

with disdain. "You're a traitor. Your only allegiance is to yourself. You're not welcome here. So leave before you have more trouble than you can handle."

"I can handle any trouble you try to give me," Mancini said arrogantly and raised his right arm to signal to his gang to get ready to attack.

The gang all took off their hoods, and Q marveled at their crude Juggalo makeup designs. Doc anxiously watched them lift their jackets and sweatshirts away from their sidearms.

"Into the breach, we go once again, my good friend," Q whispered to Doc over the radio.

"May God be with us," Doc replied and took the safeties off his weapons.

"Shall we wait here peacefully for the Keeper?" Mancini asked ominously. "Or must the killing begin now, even before he arrives?"

"Hold your fire, Q," Doc calmly whispered. "This is not our battle. Save your ammo in case we need to use it on the winners."

"Roger that!" Q replied and held his position behind a pillar.

"Noah, Madeleine, Jenny, Louis, don't panic if things get loud down here. Q and I are out of the line of fire, and we'll keep it that way unless and until Baird shows up. Do you copy?"

"Understood," Louis replied anxiously. "You guys be careful down there."

"Likewise," Doc replied. "Stay alert. We could be coming your way soon."

About that time, the conversation among the Guardians got dicey.

"We've come to see the Keeper's face when he learns his gold and silver are gone," Mancini said. "And then we'll end his reign once and for all. Why are you waiting for him?"

"We're here because we're still loyal to him!" yelled a Guardian at the front of the crowd Mancini and his gang had converged upon. "We are not like you, you filthy traitor! The moment the Keeper was locked up, you rebelled, recruited others like yourself, and stole his money wherever you could find it.

"The Keeper's cause is to rid the world of evil people who seek to cheapen and corrupt the world with evil works of art. His is a noble cause. Your only cause is to steal the Keeper's wealth and power. It is a cause so shameful you cannot even show your faces, and we want no part of it!"

"I'm more noble than you know, my friend," Mancini said in an almost conciliatory tone. "I give you one last opportunity to forsake the Keeper, who is the walking dead, and join me and my Juggalo Legion. We hide our faces merely to safeguard our anonymity in a world awash in surveillance cameras, something the Keeper never bothered to give you."

"You're wasting your breath, Mancini!" another of the Keeper's Guardians shouted. "And you have so few breaths left you should save them for your dying prayers."

"This cauldron's coming to a boil fast," Doc whispered over the radio. "At this rate, it's going to boil over before Baird even gets here ... if he gets here."

"Keep your heads down, out there!" Louis said over the radio. "Remember the plan!"

"What's the plan again, Doc?" Q asked with his predictable dark humor.

The Keeper's Guardians and Mancini's Juggalo followers began closing the distance between them. The shouting grew louder and angrier. Doc could see that Mancini was expending a lot of effort to keep all hell from breaking loose before Baird arrived.

But how will Baird get down here? Doc silently asked himself. *If he hears shouting this loud, he won't come down voluntarily. So Mancini must have a rearguard staked out in the church to close in behind Baird and prevent his escape once he starts down the stairs. He'll be trapped. That will force Q and me to join the battle in order to deliver him to the president alive.*

Doc wished he had more time to assess the situation. But Louis came on the radio.

"If you two are okay, just say okay," he said as calmly as he could.

"We're okay," Doc said loudly because the noise level in the room had at least doubled.

Doc began to wonder how much longer that would be true.

"Just keep one eye on me and your other two on what's going on around us, Q," Doc said. "If they discover us, all bets are off, and we go on offense."

"Attaboy, Doc," Q said softly. "The best defense is always a good offense."

"At that point, the only punch we will pull is taking Baird alive."

"You're kidding?!" Q asked in disbelief. "You still think he's worth the risk it will require? After everything he's put us through while we worked so hard to keep him alive for the past three years?"

"I made his daughter a promise I'd do everything possible to bring him alive, Q," Doc said. "And I intend to keep it if there's any way possible. I know it will mean something to the president too."

"All it'll mean to me is saving the cost of one bullet," Q said contemptuously.

"Be kind, Q," Doc said.

"That's as kind as I can be, Doc," Q said honestly. "You

and the president might feel you owe Baird something, but I don't."

Mancini now stood to one side of the room, and the noise became deafening as his Juggalo followers provoked one of the Keeper's Guardians by pushing him backward. Doc and Q felt another rush of air from the staircase and figured the door at the top had opened again.

"This might be Baird," Doc said over the radio.

The light at the top of the stairs cast the shadow of someone standing not far from the top. The shadow clearly showed someone frozen on the stairs. The figure pivoted … and vanished!

"What did we just see?" Q asked in disbelief.

"I believe Baird just revealed the opening to the tunnel," Doc told him. "Let's move!"

Doc and Q bounded up the stairway as quietly as possible. But their movement attracted the attention of the Guardians and Juggalos in the chamber, and they all headed up the stairs too.

"We gotta find that hidden door fast!" Doc yelled to Q.

Luckily, the door didn't close completely following Baird's hurried exit, making it easy to spot. Q reached it first and yanked it open. Doc bolted through it with Q right behind him. They stopped just long enough to try locking the door from the inside but found no lock.

"Damn it!" Doc grunted.

"Louis! Noah! You've got a crowd headed your way!" Q shouted over the radio.

"Roger that!" came from both of them simultaneously.

The tunnel was dimly illuminated, so Doc and Q never caught sight of Baird. But they heard him running well ahead of them. Behind them, they heard the shouts of Guardians and Juggalos, now united in hot pursuit.

"I should unload a few rounds at them," Q shouted through his heavy breathing as he struggled to keep up with Doc. "It'll slow them down."

"No, Q!" Doc grunted back. "It would be deafening in here, and they'll return fire. Just keep moving and move faster!"

They both knew they must be near the far end of the tunnel under Quest Publishing.

"Louis? Noah? Are you there? Do you see anyone coming out of the tunnel?" Doc shouted and hoped their answer was yes.

"Nothing at this end yet, Doc," Noah shouted back anxiously.

That made no sense to Doc. He and Q had to be nearing the end of the tunnel.

"Where's Baird?" he asked himself as he ran even faster.

"Where'd he go?" Q asked out loud.

"There must be a branch tunnel," Doc shouted. "We don't have time to look! Keep running Q! We've got to get out of here now! Noah, are you parked in back?"

"I am!" Louis answered.

"Be ready to pull the van up against the door the moment we're out!" Doc shouted, short of breath. "We've got an angry mob on our heels!"

"Roger that!" Louis answered and put the van in gear.

"I hope this tunnel ends outside the building!" Q shouted, because neither of them had any idea where the exit was.

Doc burst through the door first with Q close behind. The bright afternoon sun blinded them momentarily. Thankfully, another of Doc's hunches was right. They were outside the building, not somewhere deep within it. Louis immediately parked the van against the closed door, and he and Jenny were startled when the loud fist-pounding began on the other side of it.

"You weren't kidding about the mob behind you," he said to Doc.

"You didn't see anyone come out before us?" Doc asked again.

"No one," Louis answered.

"Damn it! There must be a branch tunnel!" Doc said, still catching his breath. "Baird thinks of every damned possibility! It's like chasing a ghost!"

"What do we do about the mob?" Louis asked Doc.

"We'll leave the van parked right where it is for now," Doc said. "They didn't know where the tunnel was either. So it's possible they have no idea where they are right now. They'll have to retrace their steps just to get back to St. John's, and they'll have no idea where we're at. Let's hop in the other van and hightail it back to the Conquest. We'll come back for this van after I've briefed the president."

"And after you and I check in with Marsha and Connie," Q added wisely.

"Oh, my gosh!" Doc blurted out. "I forgot they'll be back at the hotel soon!"

"We'll need to check in with them and let them know everyone's fine, or we'll have a lot more to worry about than Baird and Mancini," Q added.

Louis, Jenny, Q, and Doc piled into the other van with Madeleine and Noah and headed back up H Street to the Conquest. They hadn't counted on the fact that Mancini struggled with claustrophobia and never entered the tunnel. He was exiting the side door of St. John's when Q and Doc climbed out of the van. Seeing him, they scrambled into the Conquest and locked the doors as he drew a fierce-looking 45 mm Colt Python and broke into a run toward them.

"You bastards! You took my gold and silver!" he screamed and fired the Python as he ran.

Mancini fired all six rounds at Doc's driver's side window, but they couldn't penetrate the three-inch bulletproof glass. His hands shook, and he fumbled to pull more bullets from his ammo belt. Fearful that a ricocheting bullet could hit an innocent person walking or driving nearby, Doc jumped out of the Conquest and kicked the Colt out of his hand.

Q jumped out of the Conquest as Mancini charged Doc with his head down, wrapped his arms around Doc's waist, and drove him back hard into the side of the armored vehicle.

"No guns!" Doc yelled at Q, who was pulling his deadly Kriss Vector II from its holster.

Q strapped the piece back into its holster and jumped on Mancini's back as the giant of a man put Doc in a chokehold. Noah called 911 as he and the three remaining members of the team leaped from the cargo van and began pummeling Mancini to make him let go of Doc's throat. Fearing the worst when Doc began to turn blue, Jenny drew her M18, set the safety, and clubbed Mancini in the side of his head with it. He let loose of Doc, and his knees buckled slightly for a moment, but he regained his strength and was angrier than ever.

"You're all dead! Every last one of you!" he shouted at them and reached for Jenny.

"That's enough of this bullshit!" Q shouted as he drew his Kriss Vector II for a second time and stepped forward with it pointed rock-steady and directly between Mancini's eyes. "My best friend made me promise not to fire this thing. But killin' you would just be too much fun to miss. So go ahead, tough guy. Move one more muscle. Please!"

Mancini could tell by the look in Q's eyes that he meant every word he'd said. So he froze, and Q slowly returned his weapon to its holster as four D.C. police cruisers pulled to the curb and onto the sidewalk with their lights flashing.

"I don't need to kill you right now," Mancini told Doc and Q. "I'll see you again soon."

"Freeze!" one of the officers shouted while the others drew their weapons and surrounded the scene. "Which one of you is Mr. Noah Allaman?"

"I am," Noah said and stepped forward. "I called because this man assaulted my friends."

"What's your name, and what's with the makeup?" the officer asked Mancini.

"I am Lord Lorenzo Mattia Mancini!" the bald giant proclaimed with his eyes bulging.

"Lord, my ass! He's a psychopath!" Q shouted as adrenalin still had control of him.

"You're lucky the police came to your rescue!" Mancini shouted, and his mouth kept running. "I would have killed all of you with my bare hands."

The officer closest to Doc saw the darkening bruises Mancini's chokehold left on his neck and asked Doc to open his collar to give him a better look.

"He choked you?" the officer asked Doc.

"Man did he!" Doc added drama for effect. "I was blacking out when my friends pulled that crazy man off me."

"Okay, everyone," the first officer said. "Please hand me your IDs and get comfortable. If you're carrying a concealed weapon, I need your CCW also. Put Lord Manini here in cuffs," he told his partner and two other officers. "Help him get comfortable in the back of a cruiser while I call the IDs and CCWs in."

The tension eased considerably once Mancini was hand-cuffed. The officers with the IDs settled into his cruiser, tossed his hat onto the dashboard, and focused on the laptop mounted in the center of the front seat area. Everything seemed to be under control at that moment.

But in the next moment, all hell broke loose again. Mancini somehow marshaled the strength to break apart the handcuffs that bound him. With his hands free, he wheeled around and swatted away the three officers who surrounded him like bothersome flies. He managed to grab one of them by the throat as he had done to Doc, lifted him off his feet, and used him as a shield while he backed into the driver's seat of the cruiser that was supposed to deliver him to the station.

"Don't do this!" an officer shouted at him with his revolver drawn.

But Mancini merely laughed as he put the cruiser in gear and pulled into traffic. He dragged his human shield long enough to make his escape, then dropped him to the street like litter. The officer with the IDs tossed them to the sidewalk and jammed his cruiser into gear. The others did the same and gave chase while the President's Dozen stood in the middle of the sidewalk and laughed at the sight.

"Well, he's the District of Columbia's problem now!" Jenny said and high-fived her husband, Louis. "We did a fine job, didn't we?" she asked her teammates.

"All's well that ends well!" Doc said, as he often did.

"But this is only the end of a battle," Louis noted. "We still have to win the war and deliver Baird to justice."

"Real justice would put Baird and Mancini in cells next to each other," Q said.

Doc suddenly remembered that the team needed to be long gone when the Guardians and their reluctant Juggalo allies emerged from the bowels of St. John's, which could be any minute.

"Time to go, team," he said as he climbed back into the Conquest. "Last one to the Oval has to brief the president on what's happened and why Baird's still on the run. Noah, you take Louis and Jenny back for the other van, then catch up with Q and me at the White House."

"No fair, Doc!" Noah protested, while Madeleine, Jenny, and Louis just laughed and buckled in for the ride back up H Street.

"Rank has its privileges, my friend," Doc said with a shrug and a sly smile.

Technically, the White House was less than a half-mile away. Doc and Q could see it across Lafayette Square from St. John's. The drive normally takes about a minute and a half. Determined to beat the rest of the team to the Oval, Doc headed south on Madison Place NW toward Pennsylvania Avenue, where he planned to enter the White House property through the "Special Events" gate and have a quick straight shot to the West Wing entrance. But when he reached Pennsylvania Avenue, he and Q saw a sea of blue lights flashing at the east end of the block, near the 4th Street intersection.

"That's got to be more mayhem courtesy of Mancini," Q guessed.

"We better check it out," Doc said. "If it is, the president will want to know it."

Doc rolled the Conquest as far east on Pennsylvania as the police would let him. Then Q flashed U.S. Marshal badge and got Doc and himself through the police line on foot. As they approached a glut of police cruisers, it looked like at least three of them had been rammed during what was, no doubt, a high-speed chase gone wrong very quickly.

They heard Mancini's mouth before they saw his face. There were no handcuffs this time. His ankles and wrists were shackled, and he was being waddled to the back door of a cruiser when he caught sight of Doc and Q among the crowd of onlookers.

"I'm not finished with you two or with the Keeper!" he shouted maniacally as four officers tried to muscle him into the cruiser's back seat. "I'll have my day!" he screamed. "When I do, you three will suffer the worst form of vengeance!"

As soon as the officers managed to close the cruiser's rear door with Mancini still screaming inside, Doc and his closest friend headed back to the Conquest.

"Hey, Doc," Q began just as Doc knew he would, "what's the worst form of vengeance?"

"I don't know, Q," Doc sighed. "And I doubt Mancini knows."

"I bet Madeleine will know," Q said.

"Yeah," Doc said. "Good idea, Q. Ask Madeleine."

13

TRUST IS NOT AN OPTION

When Doc pulled the Conquest up to the West Wing Portico, and he and Q strode through the six-pane double doors, the president was on the phone with Tuck, telling him a car was on the way to bring him back to the White House for an emergency strategy session. The president took some comfort in knowing that Doc and his team were due back soon and counted on their input regarding possible answers to the Book's mysterious disappearance.

"We're back, Camilla!" Doc said as he and Q approached her desk with a smile.

"And not a moment too soon! The president needs to have the two of you nearby," Camilla anxiously said as she rushed from behind her desk to escort them into the Oval.

"Hello again, fellas!" the president boomed. "I just got

off the phone with Tuck, advising him that we've got a major new situation on our hands. He'll be back here in just a bit. I'll brief you as soon as Jasper joins us. In the meantime, did you get any new leads on Jonah?"

"For a moment, we thought we had him in our grasp, but he outfoxed us again," Doc admitted. "But we did manage to help the D.C. police corral Mancini. He's in custody for simple assault at the moment, unless and until we can persuade the police to charge him with something more serious. That could be a problem if his record's as squeaky clean as it was a couple of years back. At the very least, I think they can be persuaded to hold him for a psychological evaluation. Hopefully, in the meantime, we can hunt Baird down and bring him in."

"Well, we haven't had any better luck here while you were gone," the president sighed. "Some might even say we've had far worse luck."

"How so?" Doc asked, and he and Q sat up in their chairs.

"Somehow, the Book has vanished," the president said.

"When you say the 'Book,' do you mean the entire Book of Secrets?" Doc asked to be sure he understood.

"Whatever you'd prefer to call it, I've been assured it's gone," the president said solemnly as he stared out a window at the Rose Garden.

"How is that even possible?" Q asked in disbelief.

"If we knew that, we'd likely be well on our way to recovering it—or it never would have happened in the first place," the president said and returned to his chair behind the Resolute Desk. "We have hard copy documentation of much if not most of it. But the more recent of previous presidents did not create or retain hard copies of critical portions. Much of that material contained highly classified information regarding sensitive domestic and international events and operations that occurred over the last four or five decades."

"So, what's the worst-case damage?" Q asked as Cornwall entered the Oval and took a seat.

"Worst case?" the president echoed and looked at Cornwall. "Hostile foreign actors sell the details of events, dates, and names that put the lives of our intelligence assets at serious risk."

"Yep, this sounds like a real problem alright," Q said nervously.

"At the very least, if intel reaches members of Congress, I may be called to brief House and Senate committees about notes we had detailing encounters with the likes of your fabled, 700-year-old Templar Knight," the president said as he sat back and looked at the ceiling. Can't you just see clips of that on the evening news?"

"It would definitely help keep you humble, Mr. President," Doc said.

"Come what may, we must find the Book," the president said and rolled both of his hands into fists on top of the Resolute. "There is extremely sensitive information in it, of course. If it ends up in the wrong hands, it could result in irreparable harm to our nation and our allies. And on top of that, it's the singular complete source of the facts, best guesses, and beliefs every president since Washington has operated under. Our nation is richer for having it … and will be inestimably poorer if we don't recover it."

"Sounds like you can forget about a second term if this gets out," Q said cynically.

"This goes far beyond my political fate, Q," the president said as his shoulders sagged. "If we don't recover the Book, I'll go down in history as the president under whose watch the nation's heritage was erased—and our bravest intelligence assets' lives were placed at great risk. I couldn't live with that legacy."

"So, what's the latest report from Chance?" Cornwall asked, looking for a ray of hope.

"He's got a team conducting a forensic assessment," the president said. "I have no idea what that involves. But Chance didn't sound optimistic. He conducted an exhaustive search of the server before he ever advised me of the problem this afternoon."

After a crisp, two-tap knock, Tuck entered the Oval with Aubrey beside him.

"Welcome back, you two!" the president stood and boomed with a faint smile.

"What's up?" Tuck asked as he and Aubrey moved the last two chairs in the Oval near the others and sat down.

"First of all, we have not yet located Jonah," the president said. "Second of all, Chance called me back to the Situation Room right after the two of you left earlier and told me he thought the Book had vanished from Pinnacle," the president stated the problem in a nutshell.

"But he did find it, right?" Tuck shot back and moved to the edge of his seat.

"Not yet," the president said anxiously.

"How on Earth is this possible?" Tuck asked in disbelief and looked at Aubrey.

"Unfortunately, we learn more every day that in the cyber world, just about anything is possible for people with the right knowledge, hardware, and opportunity," Aubrey said. "But I know from my conversation with Chance that he's very aware of that reality, and he continually and meticulously addressed it."

"But still, it's gone," Tuck sighed.

"Aubrey, we addressed the potential long-term fallout before you and your uncle arrived," the president said. "But what's your best guess concerning the short-term downside?"

"There's no guessing involved," Aubrey said matter-of-factly. "Assuming the Book is someone's possession, that someone has more highly sensitive security information regarding our nation and our allies than you currently have, Mr. President."

"Oh, is that all?" Q feigned relief. "For a minute, I thought we had a real problem."

"Why did you bring this guy to the party?" the president asked Doc with a weak grin.

"He was your friend long before I ever met him," Doc reminded the president. "As a matter of fact, you sent him to me. I'm just trying to get even."

"It's working," the president shot back and laughed.

The sight of the president laughing eased everyone's tension, and the mood lightened.

"If you don't mind, Mr. President," Aubrey said, "I'd like to go downstairs and speak briefly with Chance again."

"No problem," the president said and led her into the elevator, initiated the scans and released the elevator, then returned to his discussion.

"Hello, Aubrey!" Chance said with obvious joy at seeing her again. "I guess you've heard about our puzzle for the day."

"I'm afraid so," she answered with a faint smile that still managed to charm Chance. "Have you made any progress?"

"Not an inch!" Chance sighed. "I'm going over everything again, but to tell you the truth, I feel like it's just a formality. It's so damn frustrating! I uploaded the week's Daily Briefing files this morning with no hint of a problem. But I haven't accessed the files in the Book for days. I've confirmed and reconfirmed that no one else has even looked at the Pinnacle directory, let alone opened or downloaded files since I last accessed any of them."

"Forgive my asking," Aubrey said hesitantly, "but for the record, have you conducted an equally thorough search of Pinnacle's backup server? There's a wild, off-the-wall chance that some set of functions and/or commands, or even an unexplained auto-recovery operation that could have possibly caused the files to migrate from Pinnacle's primary server to the backup."

"They'd be listed during the multiple scans I've conducted if anything like that had happened – but they weren't," Chance said through gritted teeth.

"Sounds to me like you've thought of everything," Aubrey told him with a confident smile. "Keep at it. I know you'll find the files. I'll check back tomorrow," she said and stepped into the elevator and was gone.

"I look forward to it," Chance whispered and studied her "special" walk into the elevator, then longingly watched the "Up" light on the elevator panel illuminate and then go out.

Chance's phone rang and ironically displayed the president's re-election campaign photo.

"Yes, Mr. President," he said. "Aubrey's on her way up, and I've made no progress."

"Chance, I'm sorry, but I'm going to have to ask you not to leave the Situation Room for the next 24 hours unless you find the Book. I know you have a small, personal quarters down there, and if you'd like, I can have someone go to your place and bring you clean clothes."

"I have some here, Mr. President," Chance replied. "And I completely understand your concern for security, sir."

"Thanks for your cooperation, son," the president said. "I'll allow your team to go home, but they'll all have to be scanned and leave their bags behind when they leave for the night."

"I'll explain it to them, Mr. President," Chance assured him.

"I know you will, and I appreciate it," the president said. "Keep up the great work, Chance! You're more valuable to me than you may feel at the moment."

"Thank you, Mr. President," Chance replied. "I appreciate hearing it, sir."

The president ended the call, turned his attention back to the Oval. "So here's today's box score," he said and pulled a pencil and writing pad from his desk. "We've lost our nation's history and haven't yet found the man who was once the individual most likely to help America lead the way in future interplanetary space exploration.

BUT, we're headed home safe and sound after an action-packed and very trying day. On the whole, I'd say today goes in our 'Win' column. It's an ugly win, but a win nonetheless!"

"If you don't mind, Mr. President, I'd like to stay behind just a while longer while Aubrey heads home now," Tuck requested. "I know she's stressed that we haven't yet found her father, and she needs to get home and relax. But I'd like just a few more minutes to discuss my brother with the four of you before I head back."

"Of course!" the president said as Aubrey stepped off the elevator.

"Dear, you're free to return to the house," Tuck told his niece. "I'll be right behind you after I discuss some other business here."

"Don't be long, Uncle," she answered, kissed his cheek, and left.

"Did you at least see Jonah?" Tuck anxiously asked Doc and Q as soon as the door closed behind his niece.

"Not actually," Doc had to admit. "But I know of no one else who would be able to elude us with such a thorough knowledge of that chamber and tunnel under St. John's. And it was clear that Mancini and his Juggalos were expecting him."

"The only lead we have left is the man who calls himself Mr. Everett Johns, who seems to be Jonah's contact at Quest Publishing on H Street," Doc said and handed

Tuck the embossed business card Madeleine brought back from her interaction with the man. "We could go back there and put some pressure on him. Maybe he'll scare easily and tell us where to find Jonah."

"I can't authorize that," the president said with a wink. "Any other ideas?"

"D.C.'s a big, crowded place. We could consult a psychic," Q suggested sarcastically. "Can we expense it?"

"I'm afraid I can't authorize that either," the president said with an exaggerated scowl.

The LED on the edge of the Resolute illuminated, and the president pressed the intercom button with a raised eyebrow.

"What is it, Camilla?" he asked. "The D.C. police are on Line One, Mr. President."

"This is the President," he boomed into the phone after pounding Line One with his meaty index finger. "How may I help you? When and where did it happen?" he asked and listened. "Are you sure?" the president gave Doc and Q an ominous look as he ended the call.

"D.C.P.D. says four guys grabbed Connie and Marsha," he told them excitedly. "It happened as they walked back to the Willard. Two detectives are waiting for you both at the hotel. Get out of here now!" the president told them.

"Well, we got our answer," Q said as he and Doc sprinted out of the West Wing Portico to the Conquest.

"What are you talking about?" Doc asked as they bolted into the hulk of an SUV, and he laid a patch of rubber on the White House circular drive.

"Now we know what Mancini meant by the worst form of vengeance," Q said angrily.

"That bastard has no idea what vengeance is about until we get our hands on him," Doc said as he raced the Conquest past a security shed, then east on Pennsylvania Avenue, where the rest of the team was waiting for them in the vans."

That left Tuck alone in the Oval with the president and Cornwall.

"Can anything else go wrong today?" he asked sadly.

"Seeing a bright side is getting harder by the minute," the president answered. "How are you holding up?"

"Okay, I guess," Tuck sighed.

"That wasn't very convincing, Tuck," the president noted with concern.

"I just feel so badly for Jonah," Tuck said. "Don't get me wrong. I understand how much chaos and death he's responsible for, Mr. President. But I remember the remarkable, civic-minded, generous man he used to be before his world came crashing down. It nearly killed me when I lost

Eleanor, and I had two years' notice that enabled me to do and say some important things before she died," Tuck explained. "I can't imagine how it must have hurt to lose Marilyn so suddenly—plus two of his daughters.

"I stuck as close to him as I could during the darkest days immediately after they were killed. I saw how he obsessed over the details of the drunk driver who caused their deaths. I knew it wasn't normal when he compiled a list of the more than 200 books the man had in the trunk of his car. Turned out, the man was a regional sales rep for a sleazy publishing house that specialized in racy dime novels and girly magazines."

"I didn't know that," the president said quietly. "That explains his Forbidden Library."

"In some alternate universe, maybe," Tuck shot back. "There's no understanding or excusing the way that tragedy broke his spirit and bent his mind. Of course, it hurts to know he's out there somewhere, alone and struggling physically and mentally. But, it's even worse knowing how much destruction, suffering, and death he's responsible for around the world."

"If anyone can find him and bring him in, Doc will, Tuck," the president said flatly. "He has the knowledge, skills, and courage to go where few others in service to our nation can go, and he gets results. He brought you in safe and silently, just as I asked him to. If there's any way possible, he'll bring Jonah in too. Now it's time you headed home and got some rest. I need you back here fresh and energetic tomorrow. Remember, we still have a missing Book of Secrets."

The suburban backed out of Tuck's driveway about 7:15 that evening. Tuck had no spring in his step as he mounted the stairs to his front door. He was emotionally exhausted and was ready for a hot shower and some of the tomato bisque and French bread he and Aubrey bought at the corner market the day before. He savored the thought of soon being in his robe, slippers, and easy chair. But before he opened the door, he heard a faint beeping. When he opened it, he instantly recoiled from the acrid black smoke that rushed out at him and the overpowering smell of something burning on the stove.

"Aubrey?! Aubrey?!" he shouted and bolted into the house with his sweater's turtleneck collar pulled up over his mouth and nose. "Aubrey! Are you here?!" he repeatedly screamed as he ran from room to room looking for her. In the kitchen, he turned off the stove, opened the window over the sink, and tossed a charred pot of blackened soup out into the yard. Done with the first floor, he charged upstairs and checked every room but did not find her.

The smoke had thinned by the time he returned to the ground floor, and he saw his niece's purse and cell phone on an end table just inside the front door. The math was easy. Aubrey had been taken! He yanked his cell phone from its holster and hit the president's speed-dial icon.

"Hello again, Tuck!" the president boomed.

"She's gone, sir! Aubrey's gone! Someone's taken her! They must have snatched her suddenly because food was still on the stove! They've got her!"

"Whoa! Slow down, Tuck," the president said. "Who's got her? Jonah?"

"No way," he said anxiously. "She would have gone willingly, and it's clear she was snatched. So I believe Mancini has her!"

"He's in custody," the president said. "At least I think he is. Hold on, and I'll check. Hold on the line, I'll be right back to you."

Tuck paced back and forth across his huge front porch, anxiously running a hand through his hair while he waited for what seemed like an eternity for the president to come back on.

"D.C. police released Mancini two hours ago," the president said. "He's got a clean record. They couldn't hold him. My guess is Mancini wants Jonah to come to him, instead of having to hunt Jonah down."

"But how will Jonah know where Mancini has her?!" Tuck asked.

"Those two used to be on the same side, Tuck," the president said. "I suppose Mancini has a few new tricks, but nothing so new that Jonah can't figure out what he's up to. With Doc and his team in the hunt, Mancini's going to get the fight he apparently wants."

"I want to be in it too," Tuck said flatly.

"I'd prefer that you left this to the professionals, Tuck," the president said.

"Well, I'd prefer none of this was necessary, Mr. President," Tuck replied, "but it is. So I have no choice. You may as well call Doc and let him know I'm on my way to join him."

"Tuck, don't do this," the president said calmly. "Tuck! Tuck!?!"

But Tuck had already holstered his Navy-issue, 9mm Beretta M9A3 under his jacket and was headed for his Lincoln. By the time the president hit his speed dial for Doc and told him Tuck was headed his way, the retired Navy captain had already launched the SUV out of the driveway. The frantic uncle raced through several red lights, and fifteen minutes later, he double-parked beside Doc's Conquest in front of the Willard InterContinental Hotel just blocks from the White House. Three police cruisers and the two rented vans were there too. A detective and three uniformed police officers questioned Doc and Q while the rest of the team and Thomas and Raymon hovered nearby. The flashing bright blue lights and the sight of Doc and his teammates leaning on the clot of vehicles in front of the hotel attracted everyone's attention within a block.

"How'd you get here so fast?" Doc asked Tuck in amazement as the detective waited for Tuck's answer with intense interest.

"I was motivated," Tuck snapped back. "What's being done to find them, Doc? When do we join the hunt?"

"This is a police matter now," Doc said. "Let them handle it."

"If you think I'm going to settle for that answer, you're out of your mind!" Tuck told him.

"Who are you, sir?" the detective asked Tuck.

"Captain Augustus T. Baird, U.S. Navy retired and senior advisor to President Prescott," Tuck said flatly and stuck his White House credential's in the detective's face but wisely elected not to mention his niece's disappearance. "Dr. Holiday's a friend of mine. Who the hell are you?"

"I'm Chief of Detectives Anderson Beaumont," the detective replied and opened his jacket just enough to clearly expose his gold badge. "This is official police business now, Captain. Thank you for your service, sir," Beaumont replied semi-sincerely.

"Thank you for yours, detective," Tuck replied flatly and returned his attention to Doc.

"Have you got all the information you need from me?" Doc asked Beaumont.

"I do—for now," Beaumont said. "Do you and the Marshal have photos of your wives?"

Doc and Q both held up photos of their wives on their

phones, and Beaumont snapped a photo of each with his own phone.

"We're on this round the clock until we find them," Beaumont said as he climbed back into the passenger side of the nearest of the three cruisers that responded to the call, and a uniformed officer slipped behind the wheel. As the cruiser pulled away, Beaumont was uploading the photos of Connie and Marsha from his phone to the D.C. Police Department's case log database.

"Maybe you're willing to roll over and let the D.C. police fumble their way around while Mancini has your wives and my niece out there somewhere, but I'm going to turn this town upside down until I find them."

"Thanks for not saying that to the detective, Tuck," Doc said and put a hand on the captain's shoulder. "It was all Q and I could do to keep from telling him the same thing."

"Welcome to the team," Q said with a broad grin that reassured Tuck he was going to be a part of the team's search effort.

"So, where do the three of you think we should begin?" Thomas asked.

"I've got what I think is a good idea," Doc answered. "But first, I'm going upstairs to grab my cane."

"What's with that cane?" Raymon asked Q as Doc

disappeared through the hotel's revolving front door. "He doesn't seem to need it."

"Well, for starters, it has a 30-inch blade inside it," Q told him. "And I know from experience that when he makes a point of having it with him, he intends to use it. So buckle up for a wild night."

"Louis and Noah, I think it's wise for us to take both vans along in case we corral a mob of Jaggaloes as we go," Q said while he walked around the Conquest and slid into the driver's seat.

"Ray and I are riding along with you and Doc," Thomas said while he stepped onto the broad running board behind Q, and Raymon did the same on the passenger side.

Doc was in his suite just long enough to grab his cane. Then he headed back down to join the team. He was midway across the lobby when he heard his name called out from the reception desk.

"Dr. Holiday! Dr. Holiday! I have another note for you, sir," said the same young man who had handed him the first note.

Doc opened the note and quickly realized it was even more important than the first one.

Dr. Holiday,

Though you're still looking for me, sources tell me you are now also looking for my beloved Aubrey, as well as Connie and Marsha.

Mancini's playing an evil, cruel game. But my sources and resources have always served me well ... and I trust they will again.

So I'm writing to suggest that you cease searching. I'm devoting all my time and energy to finding Mancini, as seems to be his wish. Once I find him, I'm confident I will also find the three ladies who mean more to me, you and Q than life itself.

I give you my word that I will succeed. When I do, I will turn myself in quietly to face the justice I deserve. As the man who gave you your life back when you had lost all hope, I ask that you trust me to do the right thing this one last time.

With all my respect and admiration,

Jonah Baird (The Keeper)

"Baird left another note," Doc told Q with a deadly serious look in his eyes as he slipped behind the wheel and handed him the neatly folded sheet of hotel stationery. Q urgently unfolded the note with shaking hands and read it.

"You're not really thinking of trusting that maniac, are you?" Q asked incredulously.

"I wish I could say no, Q," Doc said with resignation. "But if we don't find our wives soon, Jonah may be our last, best hope. The only lead I can think of is to break into Quest Publishing and find that second tunnel we know must be there. If that doesn't lead us to Mancini and his henchmen, I don't know how we'll ever find

Connie, Marsha, and Aubrey without Baird's help. Do you?"

Q simply shrugged, overcome with worry that time may be running out for justice.

"So am I prepared to trust him?" Doc asked rhetorically. "Prepared or not, trusting Baird could prove to be our last resort. If we don't find our wives soon, trust is not an option. It will be the only hope we have."

14

NO INTRODUCTION NEEDED

Doc had hatched a strategy by the time the Conquest and the two rented vans stopped in front of Quest Publishing on H Street. The strategy was far from complete. But Doc had formulated it sufficiently to convince him he had enough to lead the team into the breach.

"Q, Louis, Noah, Tuck, and Tom, grab your XRails and earplugs and follow me on foot," Doc ordered over the radio. "Jenny, you drive the Conquest. Madeleine and Raymon, you two drive the vans until we know where the tunnel leads us.

"What?!" Jenny barked back at Doc. "No way! You're not gonna bench me when the action's about to start!

"Same goes for me!" Raymon agreed.

"This isn't fair, Doc," Madeleine added. "I've only seen pictures of the tunnels. Now that I'm this close, you're keeping me out?"

"This is an order!" Doc commanded for the first time anyone could remember, which silenced the team long enough for Doc to demonstrate how a tiny transmitter built into the compass he wore on his wrist registered on the Conquest's GPS screen.

"There's no telling where the second tunnel will take us," he explained. "So track us on the screen. When we resurface, I plan to have Connie, Marsha, and Aubrey, and perhaps some Guardians with us. These vehicles must be where we need 'em, when we need 'em. Understood?"

"Understood," the trio responded as one.

"Then let's go!" Doc told Q, Louis, Noah, Thomas, and Tuck.

At the southwest corner of the building, Q climbed atop the shoulders of Doc and Louis as they bent at the waist until he had his balance. He braced himself against the brick wall as Doc and Louis stood up and made it possible for him to access the security alarm circuit box.

"I need you two at Sugar Tree when I have to paint the ceilings," Q joked as he focused on the nest of wires inside the box and identified the three primary circuits he had to disable so the team could enter the building without setting off the alarm.

"What you need is a strict diet," Doc grunted under the pressure of Q's Cody James boot.

"One—two—three!" Q counted off the circuits as he snipped their respective wires. "We're good!" he said, and Doc and Louis again bent at the waist so he could jump to the ground.

The trio moved quickly to the rear door, and Doc tried to pick the lock. After several minutes, he concluded the mechanism must have been damaged when Louis parked the van against it, and the Juggalos tried to muscle it open.

"Looks like we're going in the front door," Doc said into the radio.

Picking the front door lock was child's play, and Doc had the front door open in seconds. He tossed in a special smoke grenade he'd helped develop during his time in the SEALs, and a two-foot-thick layer of black smoke quickly rose to the ceiling, which completely obscured the surveillance cameras and gave the trio free rein to scour the first floor for the tunnel entrance.

"Follow me!" Doc said as he ran down the hallway to the Quest Publishing offices.

"I'm with you, partner!" Q assured him with Louis, Tuck, and Thomas close behind.

Doc picked Quest's lock in a heartbeat.

"We're in!" he said over the radio to the team members outside.

"The tunnel entrance has got to be here," he told those with him. "Last one in's a monkey's uncle!"

The team spread out and opened every door they came to. Each door opened to an empty or near-empty office with bare walls and no windows.

All the better! Doc thought. *We're sure to find the tunnel without too much trouble.*

"Found it!" Tuck shouted to the others from a tiny office when he discovered a heavy oak door that opened out instead of in.

By then, Doc was running on pure adrenalin. He momentarily thought about picking the lock, then impulsively threw his left shoulder hard against it and forced it open.

"BINGO!" he shouted as musty, damp air wafted up from a steep, pitch-dark stairway.

"Did anybody bring a flashlight?" Q asked hopefully.

"The shotguns have one built into the laser sight," Doc told him as he turned his on.

"What'll they think of next?" Q asked in mock amazement.

Down they went with their lights illuminating the steep stone stairway and ancient brick walls and ceiling that descended into total darkness. Doc guessed the stairs had a standard eight-inch rise. Fifty stairs down, he figured the team was about thirty feet underground.

"Madeleine, come in," he said to check radio contact with the trio outside.

"I'm here, Doc," she assured him. "You're coming in loud and clear. How about me?"

"Perfect!" he told her in happy amazement.

"Be careful, you guys," Madeleine told them. "You're picking your way through the equivalent of an underground corn maze made up of God-only-knows how many different tunnels. Some may have been planned and well-engineered, others could be quite the opposite."

"Roger that!" Louis told her as he peered down what looked to be a dark, semi-flooded dead-end side tunnel. About thirty yards farther along, he saw another tunnel just like the first—and still another one on the opposite wall, just a few more steps along the way.

"We're in what appears to be a main trunk tunnel, headed southeast," Doc announced. "But it doesn't appear to be used much. No sign of life down here yet."

"This doesn't look very promising," Tuck noted. "It sure doesn't look like anyone's been down here in a very long time. It kinda reminds me of the bowels of the *Ronald Reagan*."

"This could make an interesting chapter in that autobiography you're working on, Doc," Q wisecracked. "My Adventure in Ronald Reagan's Bowels."

"Freeze!" Doc commanded, and everyone froze in their tracks. The tunnel was as dark and quiet as a tomb, which freaked Noah out more than he let on. There had been no sign of a light switch so far. And the longer the silence lasted, the harder Noah looked for one. Doc listened intently for precisely three minutes, but heard nothing and resumed marching forward.

"Still got us in your sights, Madeleine?" Doc finally asked.

"You're about forty yards in and still headed southwest," Madeleine said softly. "See anything interesting yet?"

"Nothing," Doc replied. "Keep your earplugs around your neck and stay close together," Doc said and signaled the team to move on.

"What's the tunnel look like?" Madeleine asked.

"Old brick," Doc said. "No lights. About ten feet wide and high with an arched ceiling."

"Is it wet down there?" Madeleine asked him.

"Dry as a bone," Doc replied. "Any idea what it's for?"

"Can't be sure," Madeleine answered. "The stretch you're in sounds like it could even be a Civil War-era transport tunnel. You might find large and small chambers ahead. During the conflict, the Union stored munitions under the capital. The tunnel might simply have been used to transport ammo from point A to point B. It makes sense that Baird would pick it. Keep an eye out for hatches. They could be in the floor or overhead. And they might not be obvious."

"Do you mean this one could intersect with others?" Doc asked with some exasperation.

"Can't say," Madeleine replied. "Early on, many were simply dug as needed, with no concern for networking them. All I can reliably tell you is to keep your eyes open for surprises."

"The more things change…" Q chimed in.

"Like us, it's the nature of the beast, Q," Madeleine said with a slight smile.

In that moment, Doc saw the narrow blackness open wide to a small, dark chamber. He gathered the team close to him.

"I don't plan to spend the night in here," he said softly. "This tunnel will either take us where we need to be, or we will reach the end and make our next move."

"And what will that be?" Q predictably asked.

"I literally don't have a clue at the moment," Doc admitted. "So join me in hoping we won't need one. It appears Madeleine was right about our finding chambers down here. But I don't plan to spend the night finding out. So let's double-time it through the rest of this tunnel, however long it is. Remember what Madeleine said about hatches. Keep your eyes open, your weapons ready, and follow me! Madeleine, Jenny, and Ray, keep us on your radar and stay as close as you can," Doc commanded and led the team forward.

Approximately 200 more yards farther along, Tom was the first to catch a glimpse of a sliver of light leaking from what appeared to be a door designed to be unde-tectable … if and when it was closed properly, which it wasn't.

"Doc!" he blurted over the radio and froze in his tracks with his eyes fixed upon the light.

Doc carefully opened the door just enough to get a look beyond it while the team strained to get a look over his shoulder. With their eyes open wide and their hearts racing, they were shocked to have a bird's-eye view down into a cathedral-sized chamber, illuminated by large torches mounted to the walls, and what looked like approximately 100 Juggalos gathered around three throne-like, high back chairs, upon which sat Connie, Marsha, and Aubrey.

Doc instinctively whirled around just in time to catch Q by the shoulders as the U.S. Marshal reflexively launched himself toward the opening.

"Easy, partner …" Doc said softly as he forcefully halted his best friend's charge.

"We gotta get 'em out here now, Doc!" Q said plain-tively. "Let me go!"

"They've been here a while, Q," Doc reminded him as calmly as he could manage. "And they still look to be in good shape. Let's not do anything to change that until we know exactly what challenges we face. They don't know we're here. Let's ease in there and see what we're up against. Then we'll move. I promise you."

One by one, Doc, Q, Louis, Noah, and Tuck slid through the doorway on their bellies onto a kind of balcony that gave them a sweeping view down into the chamber. Doc used compact, lowlight binoculars to survey the chamber's perimeter for other doors. He saw none. To the left of the team, a broad stone ramp spiraled down around the chamber to the floor. The ramp had a retaining wall about two feet high that would hide the team from view as they slithered down the ramp.

"This appears to be the only way in or out," Doc said with relief. "If we surprise them, we and the women just might get out of here alive. These shotguns carry twenty-six rounds. Do the math. Used wisely, each shell can take out two or more targets. If we surprise them enough, we have a fighting chance. If we don't, the women could be used as shields, and the game is up. Don't fire until I say to. Understood?"

"Damn right, you're understood!" Q grunted over the radio. "Let's move!"

"Madeleine, keep your eyes locked on your GPS and stay on us like white on rice," Doc said. "Ray and Jenny, follow Madeleine as if she's towing you. I don't know where we're going when we leave this chamber, but we'll be going as fast as our legs will carry us. Follow me!" he commanded the team and began the long, slow descent down the ramp on his belly.

"We're near the bottom," Doc whispered over the radio. "Put your earplugs in, and on my signal, we'll jump to our feet, ready to fire if need be. That won't be easy on this steep grade. But that makes it all the more unexpected. Ready. NOW!" Doc shouted as he and the rest of the team leaped to their feet with XRail shotguns leveled at the crowd.

Doc fired two rounds at the ceiling to grab everyone's attention and send a clear message.

"First one who moves gets to heaven before me!" he shouted.

"John!" Connie shouted back. "Be careful! They've been expecting you!"

"Well, here we are!" he shouted back at everyone in the chamber. "But we intend to leave soon ... and we're taking the ladies with us!"

The crush of Guardians stood frozen for the moment. Doc quickly took stock of the situation. Best he could tell, about thirty Juggalos stood close to the women, with seventy or more others standing behind them. Doc assumed they were all armed, but he couldn't see any weapons. So the ball was in his court. And it was time to kick-off.

"Where's Mancini?!" Doc shouted at the crowd.

After a tense, five or ten-second silence, Mancini stepped forward from a few rows back.

"Like I said before, I'm Lord Mancini!" the maniac said with chest out, shoulders back. "I'm in control here!"

"I doubt that's true anymore!" Doc said and approached Mancini.

With Doc's first step, the rest of his team fanned out with their XRails leveled and ready. Surprisingly, Mancini stood silent and let Doc approach him until the XRail pressed into his chest.

"Death was already here waiting when you arrived," Mancini said. "You've merely caught up with it. I'm prepared to let it have me. How about you?" he asked. Then he turned to Connie, Marsha, and Aubrey and asked, "How about each of you?"

Doc felt a chill when he heard Mancini's words. He'd gambled that the madman wasn't crazy enough to be a martyr. But now it appeared he'd lost that bet. With his shotgun still pressed tight against Mancini's chest, Doc leaned far enough to the left to clearly see the Juggalos standing close to the women had no visible weapons pointed at their captives.

He's bluffing, Doc's brain told him. *But why? How can he expect to win? What's the point of this?*

What does it matter? his gut told him. *Get the women free and run!*

"What would you have us do, Lord Mancini!" a Juggalo shouted with a hand on Connie's shoulder. "We stand ready for your orders."

We caught them even more off guard than I'd imagined, Doc thought. *Mancini hadn't thought this out thoroughly. He must have expected Baird to show up by now. He must have hoped to talk with him. But we showed up first. And now he's trying to buy time. Don't let him. Every minute counts. Now's the time!*

A trace of terror registered on Mancini's face when Doc inserted his earplugs, and the team did the same.

"Aim high with your first rounds," Doc simply said over the radio.

That was Doc's cue for warning shots when he was about to give the order to fire. Doc then rested his XRail on Mancini's right shoulder at a 45-degree angle and fired a round that sent the madman reeling in pain and deafness. The team began firing rounds three or more feet over the Juggalos' heads. The barrage turned the room into an echo chamber of exploding noise that deafened and momentarily stunned the mob. When Doc saw weapons being raised by the Juggalos, he feared the worst was about to happen, and the women would be their first targets. Instead, those nearest the women shielded them with their own bodies, while the others began firing at Doc and his team.

Mancini still had a stunned look, and blood was flowing from his right ear as he struggled to get back on his feet. He pulled a silver-plated revolver from under his coat and pointed it at Doc. But before he could fire, Doc unleashed the XRail and killed Mancini instantly. Then Doc spun toward Connie and the other women and saw Juggalos still shielded them. Before he could look in his team's direction, a bullet tore into his left thigh, and he fell to his knees in pain.

Doc fired several more rounds from a kneeling position, and the team unleashed dozens more that filled the room with smoke and thunderous noise. Juggalos fell everywhere, while bullet ripped through Tuck's upper left arm and another creased Q's head just above his right temple. That was all Doc saw before a Juggalo rushed him from behind and kicked him to the ground, then stepped on his back and pressed a rifle barrel to the back of his head. Doc braced himself for a reunion with Mancini when he suddenly heard what he believed was Baird's voice.

"ENOUGH!" the voice shouted from the top of the ramp.

"The Keeper is here!" someone shouted from among the Juggalos. "He's alive! Praise God, the Keeper is alive!"

The Juggalo who stood over Doc backed off, allowing the former SEAL to raise his head and see Baird standing in the balcony area with his arms spread wide.

"Put your weapons away! Now!" Baird shouted to the Juggalos below. "Wipe that disgraceful makeup off your faces and act like men instead of frightened children."

To Doc's amazement, the Juggalos obeyed Baird, and the fight was over as quickly as it began. He quickly pulled his belt off and used it as a tourniquet to staunch the bleeding in his leg. Then he struggled to his feet, checked Q's wound, and stopped the bleeding in Tuck's left upper arm with a couple of zip ties from his vest.

"Anybody else hit?" he called out to his team.

"None of us," Noah said. "But there's a bunch of them who are … and I believe they're all beyond being helped."

It was only then that Thomas felt the searing pain of having been shot clean through the lower right side of his ribcage and collapsed.

"Doc, I think I've been hit," he managed to say before he passed out from the loss of blood.

Doc ran to him, checked his pulse and his wound, and then used his own shirt to staunch the bleeding. While Doc was focused on his teammates, Baird had descended into the chamber and was mobbed by exuberant ex-Juggalos who renewed their vow as Guardians the moment they first caught sight of him on the balcony above them.

One of them untied Connie, Marsha, and Aubrey. As the three of them stood up and rubbed their aching wrists, Baird cautiously approached his long-estranged, youngest daughter with a look in his eyes and a love in his heart only fathers know.

"Papa?" Aubrey uttered softly. "Papa, can you ever forgive me?"

"Let's forgive each other, my darling daughter," Baird said through tears and embraced her tightly. "Let's forgive each other."

Still holding Aubrey close, Baird looked about him at the death and devastation and was wracked with knowing he was responsible for all of it. He then spotted Doc kneeling over Thomas and called to him.

"Are you alright, Doc?" he asked urgently. "How is he?"

"I'm okay, and he will be," Doc answered. "But we have to get him to a hospital, quick," he said into the radio. "Are you hearing all this, Madeleine?"

"I heard everything loud and clear, Doc!" Madeleine assured him and put the Conquest into gear. "I see where you are. But I have no idea where you'll emerge. Get moving so we know which way to go."

"Noah, Louis, give me a hand getting these guys out of here," Doc said. "Let's move out!"

"We don't have far to go," Baird said.

"We?!" Doc shot back at him. "You're going with us?"

"Of course," Baird told him. "I won't let my daughter go until the law says I must."

"And I won't let you two go again 'til the day I die," Tuck said and hugged them both.

"Well, I hope that day's a long way off," Baird told his kid brother with a broad smile.

Connie rushed to Doc and wrapped him in her arms. Marsha embraced Q with love and relief and kissed the wound at the side of his head. Louis and Noah fell into step with the group. And Doc could only shake his head in amazement as six Guardians lifted Thomas above their heads and followed Baird and everyone else back into the tunnel. Less than ten minutes later, they all stepped through a steel door into a modern, well-lighted chamber.

"We're out," Baird announced.

"We are?" Doc asked, though he knew Baird must be right.

"Oh, yes, we are!" Baird said with a broad grin. "And I think you might be quite amazed by who's waiting for us outside. Just follow me up these stairs, and we'll be outside momentarily."

"Madeleine, are you still hearing this?" Doc asked.

"Sure am," she replied. "According to your tracker, I'm a quarter-mile away."

"Can you see anyone waiting for us?" Doc asked her hopefully.

"Not really," she said. "But unless your tracker's wrong, you're in for quite a surprise!"

"Well, at least call 911 and get four ambulances for us,

would you please?" he asked.

"Four ambulances! Are you sure everyone's going to be alright?" she shrieked.

"Fortunately, it's not as bad as it sounds," Doc assured her.

Still, Doc remained dumbfounded. He had no idea where they must be.

"Who's waiting for us, Jonah?" he anxiously asked Baird.

The man of many surprises merely smiled at Doc and unlatched another steel door at the top of the short flight of stairs.

"Trust me, Doc," he chuckled. "When you see him, there'll be no introduction needed."

With that, Baird held the door open and let Doc and Connie step through it first.

"Ha, ha, ha, ho my god!" Connie burst into laughter.

Doc froze, blinked several times, and desperately tried to process the sight before him.

"Was I right, or was I right?" Baird asked mischievously as he stepped between Doc and the gigantic white Georgia marble statue of Abraham Lincoln, seated majestically in the center of his wondrous memorial.

Connie laughed, the rest of the team hooted and hollered, and Doc was speechless. Madeleine laughed hysterically when she caught sight of the crowd gathered around the statue, steered the Conquest up the memorial's broad granite steps, and stepped on the gas. National Park Service cruisers surrounded the rented cargo vans Jenny and Raymon sat waiting in on Lincoln Memorial Circle Northwest, flashing lights and all, right at the start of rush hour.

"You better call the president and get this straightened out quick," Connie giggled.

"Good morning, Mr. President," Doc said when POTUS picked up. "Can you talk?"

"To you, of course!" the president boomed as he wiped the shaving cream off his face. "But I'm due in my Daily Briefing in twenty minutes. So please keep it short."

"We've got Connie, Marsha, Aubrey … and Jonah," Doc said with great satisfaction.

"That's excellent news!" the president shouted. "Is everyone alright?"

"Mostly!" Doc said. "A few scratches here and there. But nothing fifteen minutes in the E.R. can't fix. I'm hoping you can call Walter Reed and explain to them that we need to meet with you following your briefing."

"Done!" the president boomed. "See you then!" he bellowed happily and ended the call.

The visit to Walter Reed took forty minutes more than

Doc's estimated fifteen. Doc called the president as soon as the team was ready for the trip to the Oval.

"Hello, Doc!" Camilla said cheerfully. "The president's still in his Daily Briefing. But he asked me to have you use the H Street Entrance. They're expecting you."

"Great!" Doc said with false enthusiasm. "See you in a few," he said, dreading the thought of another tunnel.

15

TOO BAD TO BE TRUE

Doc used the twenty-minute drive to process the president's Daily Briefing lasting more than an hour. Barring the threat of a nuclear war, there was no explaining such a long session ... unless, of course, the president had opted for full disclosure concerning the missing Book of Secrets.

"So, has the Situation Room solved their mystery yet?" Aubrey asked Doc cryptically because her father was in the Conquest with them.

"I don't believe so," Doc said honestly. "But I'm sure they soon will."

Baird reached across from his seat to Aubrey's and grasped her hand.

"I'm absolutely thrilled to have you here, sweetheart," he told her. "But I never dreamed you'd get involved in my affairs to this extent."

"What did you think I'd do, Father?" she asked gently. "I'm not the type to sit at home and hope that others find you and bring you back to me safe and sound."

"And you should be proud, Jonah," Tuck told him, and winced at the sharp pain he got in his patched-up left arm when he leaned in that direction. "Frankly, she's already been a big help in a high-priority effort at the White House."

"Really?" Baird replied. "Anything you can talk about?"

"Unfortunately not," Aubrey quickly said and changed the subject.

"What will become of you, Father?" she asked Baird.

"I don't know," he said. "The only plan I have is to spend every moment I possibly can with you and Tuck until we know more about my fate. And whatever my fate may be, I already know the biggest part of it: You're home again, where you belong. God willing, I'll be there with you someday. In the meantime, I have peace of mind of knowing the smartest businesswoman in the world is running whatever is left of my business enterprises, from here to Mars."

"You have a lot of faith in me, considering we haven't spoken in more than nine years."

"I've followed your education and career more closely than you can imagine, my dear," Baird assured her. "And believe me when I say I'm quite comfortable with the arrangement!"

"Thank you, Father," Aubrey said gratefully. "I'll make you proud."

"You already have, my dear," Baird told her. "You've made me proud indeed."

Doc carefully pulled the Conquest into the entryway of a nondescript brick office building across a barricaded alley from 1510 H Street and stopped at the window just inside.

"Welcome back, Doc! Long time, no see!" Secret Service Agent Kirklind Dixon said with a massive grin. "Are you here on business or pleasure?"

"You know me, Kirk," Doc said and smiled back. "Business is my pleasure—and pleasure is my business. The folks in the cargo vans are with me. The president invited all of us. We'll need a close screening for one at the other end before we enter the building, Kirk."

"No problem, Doc. I'll call and let 'em know right now," the tall, muscular agent said. "Tell POTUS, Big Kirk said, 'Hey.' I reckon I'll see you again on your way out."

"I hope so," Doc said and headed down into the tunnel that leads to a small parking area beside a basement entrance to the East Wing of the White House.

Two agents outside the entrance waved Baird through the metal detector, then wanded him before a careful pat-down.

"He's clean," one of the agents told Doc formally and waved them on.

"Sorry, Jonah, but you've taught us to be vigilant," Doc said with an unapologetic tone.

"No offense taken," Baird said with a tilt of his head. "I'm sure I've earned it."

Moments later, Camilla led Doc and the others into the Oval, then shared tea and conversation with Connie and Marsha at her desk.

"Come in!" the president boomed his loudest yet. "Seeing you all always lifts my spirits, and believe me, I need that more than ever this morning. Are you alright, Tuck?" he asked when he saw his senior advisor's arm in a sling.

"It's nothing, really, Mr. President," Tuck assured him. "I barely feel anything."

"Wish I could say the same," the president said with a forced chuckle.

"Rough Daily Briefing?" Doc asked

"Very!" the president said. "This China sub debacle is driving me nuts. The NSA and CIA are like dogs with a bone concerning what I intend to do about the photos they gave me last week. But since then, what have they and the NRO brought me about that mess that's new? Bupkis! Yet, they act as though they're ready to start World War III over it."

"Have you told them the images have disappeared along with the Book of Secrets?"

"Not yet," the president said. "Fortunately, I got new copies in the data from today's briefing. The Situation Room has them now."

"Can we please see them on a large screen again?" Aubrey asked.

"Certainly," the president said. "Please hold my calls and enjoy your tea, Camilla!" he boomed into the intercom.

"What will I do in the meantime?" Baird asked earnestly.

"You still have your security clearance," the president said with a shrug and led them all into the elevator.

"Wow! It's like a homecoming!" Chance whooped when they stepped into the Situation Room. "Have you come to find the missing Book of Secrets for me?" he asked with a heavy sigh.

"They have not," the president said. "But they would like to see the cursed 094A images we got this morning, Chance," the president said and led the team into a viewing room.

Chance purposefully punched one key on his keyboard and joined them.

"The first six are of the subs we've known about since 2007," Chance said as he clicked a tiny remote control, and the slide show began. "The twelve after that are individual and group shots of the new subs."

The team sat quietly and took in the images.

"What altitude were these taken from?" Raymon asked.

"I can't disclose that," Chance said. "But it was more than 100 miles."

"That's absolutely amazing," Raymon remarked. "If I weren't looking at them with my own eyes, I'd say it was impossible for the photos to be so clear and detailed."

"I know," the president grumbled. "It's ridiculous the way we can take such unbelievably clear photos from more than 100 miles away, but bank ATMs take such miserable ones inches away."

"I'm not complaining about ATM picture quality," Aubrey chimed in. "They were good enough to bring my father home to me," she said as she hugged Baird's arm tight again. "But I understand what you're saying, Mr. President. If someone had told me our satellites could produce this quality regardless of the atmospheric conditions, I'd say it was too good to be true."

"Well, that's the end of the show, folks," Chance said. "Please leave your thoughts and comments at the door and pay as you exit."

The president deftly stepped up to Jonah and put a hand on his old friend's shoulder.

"Jonah," he said quietly, "the FBI is waiting in the

garage to discreetly take you into custody. They've been instructed to give you and Aubrey time and space to say your goodbyes for now—or she can ride along with you if that's what the two of you would like. I wish you well, Jonah, and I would appreciate an opportunity to talk with you, one friend to another, very soon. Until then, I will pray that God and the justice system will be kind to you, but also fair and just to everyone touched by your actions these last few years."

"You and I will be praying the same prayer," Baird told his friend. "I regret the way the last several years unfolded, and I will also pray for an opportunity to somehow make everything up to you and the world someday. Goodbye for now, Donald—my president."

"Vaya con dios, Jonah—my good friend," the president said with a sad smile.

The team stopped just long enough at Camilla's desk to say their goodbyes and have Connie and Marsha join them. Then Doc led them and Aubrey, Baird, Thomas, Raymon, Louis, Jenny, Madeleine, Noah, and Q on the long walk to the basement exit of the East Wing. Jonah asked Doc to stop about twenty feet from the exit.

"I need a moment alone with Doc while you and the others go on ahead, Aubrey," he told his daughter softly as he held her hands, and she began to cry. "I want you to remember me like this, in the White House, not outside those doors with the FBI. I know you understand."

"I do, Papa," Aubrey said and wiped her tears before she kissed his cheek and gave him one last hug until the day she would be able to give him another.

When Aubrey and the others exited the basement, Doc put a hand on Baird's shoulder and locked eyes with him.

"I think I now know where it went off the tracks for you, Jonah," he said quietly. "And I guess I'll never know the hell your demons dragged you and the rest of the world through. But I do know you saved a lot of lives tonight, including Connie's and mine. And I want you to know I'll be forever grateful."

"Strange, isn't it?" Baird said with a slight smile. "If my life hadn't, as you say, left the tracks, you and I would have likely never have met, and we would have both been lesser men for it. You may well be right to believe that everything happens for a reason, Doc."

"I'm sure it does, Jonah. Even things as sad as this," Doc said with a slight smile of his own as he led Baird to the exit and into the custody of the FBI.

Doc then walked the long, narrow tunnel back to the H Street entrance, where the rest of the team waited for him. He chuckled when he saw Connie behind the wheel of the hulking, seven-ton Conquest. And he quickly climbed in beside her and kissed her passionately to the cheers of the others on board.

"Get a room you two, would ya'!" Q wisecracked from two rows back.

"Sounds like a good idea to me!" Marsha said with feeling and happily kissed Q.

"Well, I can see the two of you have come through this alright," Doc chuckled.

"How about you?" he gently asked Aubrey, who sat directly behind Connie. "Are you going to be okay?"

"I'm fine, Doc. Really," she assured him. "I'll never be able to thank all of you for the miracle this night has been. I'm far, far happier than I might appear at the moment, and I'm doing just fine!"

"Well then, let's get you and Tuck back home," Doc said.

"I left all the windows open," Tuck laughed in the back row. "So, the place should be as fresh as a daisy!"

"Aubrey, I need to ask you about something Chance said tonight," Madeleine said on Aubrey's right.

"Please do," the MIT Computer Science and Aerospace Technologies Ph.D. replied.

"He said if he had only heard about the quality of those submarine pictures without having actually seen them, his opinion would be that the story would be too good to be true," Madeleine reminded her.

"Under the same conditions, I would probably agree with him," Aubrey said.

"But the president has yet to receive any additional photos," Madeleine replied. "Does that seem odd to you?"

"Well, having no additional photos doesn't seem as odd as having no additional intelligence about the photos we do have," Aubrey answered thoughtfully. "After several days of analysis, it's hard to understand why no one's been able to provide important answers the president urgently needs—whether it's about how the additional subs were built so secretly or why we were able to so easily capture them in plain sight—but only once, and only for a few moments. It's got to be driving the president crazy."

"And on top of all that, the president's Book of Secrets is missing!" Q interjected. "How's that for a bad week at the office? Or should I say, in the office? And just when he's about to run for re-election."

"It is a hell of a rat's nest of unfortunate coincidences," Noah said from the seat beside Tuck. "I'm glad we don't have to solve it."

"It just doesn't add up," Madeleine agonized out loud. "It doesn't make sense."

"Maybe you should use that Doyle fellas equation on it," Q told her half in jest. "You know, 'once you've eliminated the impossible, whatever remains, however improbable, must be the truth.'"

"Why, Q!" Madeleine gushed. "You've actually memorized it! That's terrific!"

"Sure I have," he answered her. "You made a believer out of me way back in Israel. But I'm still not sure I completely understand it."

"Me either, Q," she replied. "I only know that it works … if and when you can truly eliminate the impossible."

That's when Connie stopped the Conquest in front of Tuck's house and let out a sigh.

"Well, I know Aubrey and I aren't going to be able to fall asleep for a while," Tuck said. "Does fresh-brewed coffee and homemade pastries sound good to anyone else?"

Connie parked the SUV and shut it off.

"Coffee and pastries it is!" Doc said. "Follow me, team!"

"I'll get the coffee and pastries started if you and your team will close all the windows I left open," Tuck told Doc with a laugh.

"Sounds like a deal," Doc replied. "And it'll be easier than figuring out who's sitting in the black sedan two doors down … or who was driving the one that followed us here."

"I didn't notice," Tuck said nervously.

"I did," Doc said. "These fellas are sloppy. It pains me to say it, but they must be Feds."

Fifteen minutes later, Tuck poured the coffee, Aubrey passed out the pastries, and the shadowy figures still sat in the dark sedan two doors down. Doc sat in an easy chair that gave him a clear view out the front window to the sidewalk. It was an old habit he still had use for.

"The coffee and pastries are wonderful!" Marsha said, "but I will scream if anyone tries to talk business while we have this chance to enjoy one another's company."

"You took the words right out of my mouth," Connie said with her famous smile.

"Well, I, for one, don't even feel like talking right now," Jenny said. "I'd be happy just to lay back in Louis's arms and watch a good TV movie. Is there anything good on?"

Tuck grabbed the TV remote and turned on his 50-inch flat-screen just as a History Channel made-for-TV movie began. Everyone groaned and laughed, and Tuck clicked off the TV when the "President's Book of Secrets" appeared on the screen.

"It's a curse!" Louis shouted whimsically. "Jenny and I haven't had a chance to cuddle in front of the TV in weeks!"

"Well, that's something I don't sure want to talk about," Q said. "Is anybody up for a quick game of cards or an easy board game?"

. . .

A pinnacle game broke out and distracted everyone but Aubrey, Madeleine, and Tuck. The three of them got comfortable in a corner of the living room and sipped coffee while they tossed facts and questions to one another. After about fifteen minutes of talking, Tuck settled back in his easy chair and sighed.

"We've said so much about the photos and the Book today," he groaned in desperation. "What haven't we said yet?"

"Well, we've said a lot about the photos being too good to be true," Madeleine told him. "But what if they're too bad to be true?"

"What?" he shot back at her.

"Aubrey, you've done a lot of research about cybersecurity, right?" Madeleine asked.

"I sure have," Aubrey agreed.

"Am I wrong, or is it true that digital images can be altered—manipulated—and you'd never know it unless you have access to the original, unaltered files?"

"That's very true," Aubrey said with renewed enthusiasm.

"Hold it right there!" Tuck said excitedly. "I hope you don't actually believe that the Director of National Intelligence and the heads of the CIA and the Office of

Naval Intelligence knowingly gave the president altered images of those submarines."

"I'm not saying I believe it or that it's even probable, Tuck," Madeleine replied. "I'm just saying it's not impossible, and the president—and for that matter, the Situation Room—would never know it."

"That's crazy!" Tuck said and slid to the edge of his seat. "What motive could they possibly have to mislead the president?"

"One of the oldest motives in the history of our nation, Tuck," Madeleine said calmly. "None other than George Washington wrote in 1799 that the secret to peace was to make our nation's enemies believe, 'that offensive operations, oftentimes, is the surest, if not the only (in some cases) means of defense.'"

"What the hell is that supposed to prove?" Tuck snapped at her. "He was talking about real means of defense, not made-up threats to the nation!"

"And what if factions in the leadership of our military and our intelligence community secretly agreed that one sure way to invigorate and expand our offensive operations would be to convince the president that it was an urgently needed 'means of defense'?"

"That's just not possible!" Tuck said on the verge of anger.

"Are you sure?" Madeleine challenged him. "Unless we can be certain it's impossible, however improbable you think it is, it just may be the truth ... and you just heard your niece confirm that no one but those who gave the images to the president can be certain they are real. Which, according to Arthur Conan Doyle's equation, could mean the president has what I would call a 'Reverse LBJ' on his hands."

"What the hell's a 'Reverse LBJ'?" Tuck said with escalating exasperation.

"During the 1950s, a Soviet hoax sparked widespread fears that America was on the losing side of a bomber gap," Madeleine explained. "Then in 1968, when satellite photography came into its own, the U.S. intelligence agencies assured President Johnson they were certain no new ICBM complexes had been established in the USSR."

"I know that!" Doc told her defiantly. "How do you know it, and what does it prove?"

"I'm a nerd," she said matter-of-factly, "a history nut who used to be a researcher in the Vatican Secret Library, where I learned a lot of things no one's particularly interested in nowadays. That's where I dug out a remark President Johnson made at a gathering in 1967. I'm willing to bet it's quoted somewhere in the missing Book of Secrets."

"So, what did LBJ say?" Tuck asked with the beginnings of genuine interest.

Madeleine pulled out her phone and accessed a file.

"I've been mulling this statement over in my head for a couple of days now," she explained. "He said, 'We've spent 35 or 40 billion dollars on the space program. And if nothing else had come out of it except the knowledge that we gained from space photography, it would be worth ten times what the whole program has cost. Because tonight we know how many missiles the enemy has and, it turned out, our guesses were way off. We were doing things we didn't need to do. We were building things we didn't need to build. We were harboring fears we didn't need to harbor.'

"So what do you think some of our more hawkish military brass and intelligence chiefs might be capable of if they somehow managed to convince one another that we're not building things we need to build ... and we're not harboring fears we need to harbor?"

Without another word—and with thoughts of the men in those black sedans Doc warned him about—Tuck pulled out his own cell phone and hit the president's speed-dial icon.

"Mr. President, I'm terribly sorry to bother you at such a late hour," he said sheepishly, "but unless you're in your pajamas, we'd like to briefly speak with you in person again tonight."

"Thank you, Mr. President," Tuck said with relief. "We'll be there shortly."

Tuck bounded over to the card game, announced the new White House trip, and he and his two co-conspirators led the confused members of the team back out to the Conquest.

"Your turn to drive," Connie told her husband and gladly took the front passenger seat.

"Hey!" Tuck shouted to the fellas in the parked black sedan. "We're on our way back to the White House, in case you need it for your report."

Tuck then climbed into the Conquest, and the team headed north.

"The president said to use the H Street tunnel again, so no one tips the media about such a late-night visit," he told Doc as the SUV rumbled across the Arlington Memorial Bridge and swept past the Lincoln Memorial once again.

"I'll never think of that place the same ever again," Q told the team.

"Neither will we!" they replied in unison and laughed.

Doc stopped at the window just inside the building again.

"Whatchu doin' workin' so late, Doc?" Secret Service Agent Kirkland Dixon asked with a huge grin.

"Me? I'm having fun," Doc said with his own grin. "What are you doin' here so late?"

"Overtime and shift premium," Dixon laughed. "I got a new baby on the way!"

"Congratulations!" the team shouted out.

"Thank you, folks!" Dixon said with a huge laugh.

"Boy or girl?" Connie asked.

"A little girl!" Dixon gushed. "Already got two boys."

"Pick a name yet?" Connie had to ask.

"Melania!" Dixon said happily. "But don't tell the president. I want to do that myself."

"It'll be our secret!" Connie promised him as Doc headed the Conquest down the ramp to the White House East Wing.

"It's nice to know a new, happy secret for a change," Connie told Doc with a smile.

"Roger that!" he replied, then reached out and squeezed her hand.

The president was waiting for them at the basement entrance and led them to the Oval.

"This must be important," he said to Doc as they walked through the basement toward the West Wing."

"That's what I told Tuck when he announced that you were expecting us," Doc replied.

"You mean he hasn't discussed it with you?" the president asked in surprise.

"Not a word," Doc said. "I just know it's about something he and Madeleine and Aubrey discussed among themselves at his house tonight."

"Yeah, we were just playin' cards," Q chimed in. "I was winning too. But don't worry, no money was involved, Mr. President."

"No matter what, I know I can always count on you, Q," the president said with a hearty laugh and kept walking.

When they reached the Oval Office, the president thought a moment before taking his seat.

"Tuck, if this has anything to do with those 094A photos, we might as well take this down to the Situation Room right now. Chance is still there around the clock, and if you have something that might help him, I know he'll want to hear it."

"Lead the way, Mr. President," Tuck said, and the team joined the president in the elevator.

Chance greeted them in a baggy sweatshirt, cut-off jeans, and flip-flops.

"Sorry I didn't dress up for you all, but these are not my normal business hours," he said with his boyish smile. "What's up?"

After he and the team got comfortable in a soundproof room, Madeleine walked him through a short version of her "Reverse LBJ" scenario.

"That's an extremely interesting theory, for sure," he

said and ran a hand through his wavy, uncombed hair. "But as you said yourself, there's no way we can be sure of whether or not the photos have been altered. It's scary to know how easy it would be to make six real subs appear to be a dozen or more of them. But the scariest part of your theory is the thought that American patriots might actually be capable of doing it.

"And as far as I'm concerned, the very worst part is that none of this helps me in my search for the missing Book of Secrets," he said with sagging shoulders.

"I'm not too sure of that either," Aubrey said in measured words.

"What's that supposed to mean?" Chance asked incredulously.

"Let's quickly run through that mystery," Aubrey suggested with the excitement that comes when a mental light goes on. "Pinnacle is not networked."

"Correct," Chance simply said.

"It's completely off the grid," Aubrey said.

"Correct," Chance confirmed.

"No one but you accessed the Book of Secrets for more than a week prior to its disappearance," Aubrey continued.

"Correct again," he said, growing weary and wary of the repetition.

"And you did not take it?" Aubrey asked for the record.

"Of course not!" Chance said disdainfully.

"Then it must still be in Pinnacle," Aubrey said.

"But it's not!" Chance said with full-blown anger and frustration.

"But it must be," Aubrey insisted.

"But it's not!" Chance nearly shouted. "And insisting otherwise won't make it so."

"But finding it will!" she said confidently.

"Then show me how or shut up about it!" Chance snickered.

At this point, they had the full attention of the president and the entire team.

"Lead the way," Aubrey said with an impish smile that only upset Chance more.

The entire team now gathered around Pinnacle, eager to see who would win this verbal prize fight.

"Pinnacle's the most advanced computer our nation has, correct?" Aubrey asked.

"Correct!" Chance sighed; she was wearing him down.

"In fact, Pinnacle is really two of the most advance computers, correct?" she pressed him.

Chance now just nodded yes, and looked as though his defeat was at hand.

"Have you rebooted them?" Aubrey asked.

"Twice," Chance sighed.

"Separately, one at a time, or simultaneously?" Aubrey asked optimistically.

"Sim-mul-tan-eous-ly!" Chance said as a mental light of his own came on.

"What data is on Pinnacle One?" Aubrey continued the drill.

"Everything!" Chance now matched her stride.

"And what data is on Pinnacle Two?" she predictably asked next.

"Everything!" Chance blurted at her, unsure of why she made him.

"And they continually hand it all back and forth to each other at the speed of light, correct?" she pressed him further.

"Correct!" he nearly screamed.

"How long would it take to download everything on Pinnacle One to discs?" she asked.

"Maybe twenty minutes, max!" Chance said. "But why would we do that? It's all already backed up on Pinnacle Two. That's the point of having two of them."

"Yes, it is," Aubrey agreed. "But humor me, please."

The president played host and poured the team and himself coffee while Chance humored Aubrey—and she fussed with his wavy hair, and they all waited for the backup to be complete.

"It's done!" Chance announced as he checked out his in a nearby dark monitor.

"Okay, now shut Pinnacle One completely down," Aubrey told him.

As Chance shut it down, his mental light suddenly burned even brighter, and he was beginning to see it.

"Now let's look at the files in the Pinnacle Two directory," Aubrey told him.

"It's here! It's right here!" Chance shouted in sheer excitement and massive relief.

"What is?" the president urgently asked because he didn't dare assume the answer.

"The Book! It's right here!" Chance laughed.

"It's been there the whole time," Aubrey said softly and winked at Madeleine. "Well, actually, it's been there, and then it's been on Pinnacle One, and then it's been there again, going back and forth from one to two and back again at 299,792,458 meters per second. And because there was only one file instead of two, it couldn't be seen in either directory with the naked eye, nor could it be printed out."

"Well, download us a copy right now!" the president called out.

"That's a violation of protocol, Mr. President," Chance reminded him.

"Download that file right this minute," the president boomed. "That's an order, Corporal!"

"Yes, sir!" Chance happily replied and downloaded the file to a monster flash drive and handed it to the president. "I would appreciate a receipt for that when you can get it to me," he sheepishly told the president.

"I'll have Camilla take care of it when she gets in," the president assured him with a smile.

"But how did that happen?" Tuck blurted out in the interest of avoiding it in the future.

"Machine Learning," Chance replied.

"You mean like artificial intelligence?" Tuck asked, for clarity.

"Not quite, but very close to it," Aubrey explained. "I suspect that sometime over the last week or so, Pinnacle began to question discrepancies it believed it saw in the data you were uploading, Chance. I believe the submarine photos could have been the proverbial straw that broke the camel's back and caused Pinnacle to devise a means of preserving the integrity of the files it knew were credible while it continued to receive files it suspected were not credible. My guess is you will find there are conflicting data sets related to the locations and the maximum speed and range of the 094As," Aubrey continued.

"Knowing that—and knowing its primary mission is to ensure the integrity of the files I give it to safeguard," Chance stepped in to round out the explanation, "Pinnacle could very well have taken matters into its own cyber hands and created a kind of surety protocol in the name of preserving the President's Book of Secrets."

"Mr. President, I believe you need to have a thorough list of very pointed and powerful questions for Armstrong when she arrives for your Daily Briefing in a few hours," Tuck told him. "I'll be happy to stay and help you with that list if you'd like."

"I'd appreciate that very much, Tuck," the president boomed. "And I believe the rest of you would appreciate finally getting to bed sometime soon, am I right?"

"I'm willing to bet a transcript of this morning's Daily Briefing will end up in the Book," Doc said to the president as he shook his hand goodbye and led the team—minus Tuck—back to the East Wing garage exit.

"That's a remarkable bunch, Tuck," the president said with a hand on the shoulder of his Senior Advisor for Strategic Military Affairs. "Now that there's more than six members, I should probably stop calling them my Dozen."

"What do you think you'll call them instead?" Tuck asked, knowing he and his niece were de facto members.

"I don't know what I'll call them," the president said thoughtfully. "I'm just thankful I can call them whenever the nation faces a challenge too great for mere mortals."

EPILOGUE

The nation may never know the extent to which the "President's Dozen" played a role in President Prescott's re-election—and thereby influenced global events in untold ways. After all, there's little record that the team even exists. But like so much that goes on in the name of defending and preserving our nation's security interests, their sacrifice, courage, and impact remain wrapped in secrecy and can only be found in a book most Americans think is a mere legend rather than a reality.

But it's clear that the "President's Book of Secrets" and the "Keeper," Jonah Baird, are again right where they belong, thanks to Doc and his team. The secrets chronicled in the Book are a priceless guide to the unvarnished truths that help presidents better understand the nation's past and more intelligently envision its future. How ironic it is that although the team operated in total secrecy, they could have no greater legacy!

In the days following this latest of their great adventures, Doc came to realize that even if he finished his autobiography one day, he'd never be granted permission to publish it. He was fine with that. It made him smile to think that he was living a life filled with people, places, and adventures that most folks could hardly imagine—let alone believe existed.

So the only personal, uncensored account of the team's exploits was being authored by Madeleine, who faithfully devoted a lot of time and thought after each mission to chronicle obscure and puzzling questions and observations that resisted explanation.

For instance:

- How did Jonah Baird so quickly know so much about the team's whereabouts and plans?
- Why do so many abandoned tunnels still exist under our nation's capitol?
- What scientific and engineering breakthroughs and nightmares does the future of artificial intelligence hold for America and the world?
- Who is Everett Johns, really?

Madeleine knew that the Grand Mysteries might never be solved. That complication never deterred her. In fact, she saw it as the primary reason she should invest the time and energy and never stop hoping for the answers because, after all, everything happens for a reason.

. . .

THE END

BOOKS OF THIS SERIES IN ORDER

Find all books of this series in order here:

https://www.prestonwilliamchild.com/books

SPECIAL OFFER

Want to read some of my books for FREE?
Available for a limited time only. To download them, go
to my

Free Starter Library

ABOUT THE AUTHOR

I'm an South-African author of Action & Adventure novels. I've been self-publishing since 2013. I've written more than fourty novels in different series. For more information about me and my books please visit my website

http://prestonwilliamchild.com

Made in the USA
Las Vegas, NV
18 July 2023

74939418R00167